Christmas at the Hog and Frog

Books in *The Netties Knit Shop Series* by CB Landy:

Secrets of the Wool
A Tisket A Tasket
Died with Flowers

Seasonal stories:
Lost Angels – A short story – kindle only
Christmas at the Hog and Frog

Website: **https://www.cblandyauthor.com/**

Christmas at the Hog and Frog

A Netties Knit Shop Seasonal Novella

CB Landy

Copyright © 2022 CB Landy

Revised edition.

ISBN 978-0-473-61494-2 (Kindle)

ISBN 978-0-473-61493-5 (softcover)

Cover art design by Rox Orange

"The holiday season is a perfect time to reflect on our blessings and seek ways to make life better for those around us."

– Anonymous

Contents

November

Bob Fletcher

The phone chimed to alert Bob a text had arrived. He put his book down and glared at it. Usually he would have ignored it until he was ready, although he had to admit that sometimes he forgot. It caused two of his children to worry and the third just got angry with him.

He looked over to the wall clock and was surprised to see a good hour and a half had passed since he'd started reading. This wasn't good. He needed to keep moving, especially now after being a victim of a bicycle hit and run, resulting in a fractured femur. He was no spring chicken, as the doctor kept reminding him, and the phrase 'use it or lose it' was bandied about at each check-up.

Pushing himself out of the armchair, Bob felt a pain travel up his leg, and into his hip. He needed to walk it out, but slowly at first. He limped over to the kitchen table and picked up the phone to read the text. It was his youngest, Diane, wanting to know what he wanted for Christmas.

"Christmas!" Bob spluttered in surprise. His head moving to the calendar on the wall, it was only the 20th of November, why would she be bothering him about presents now?

He put the phone down and walked out to the back garden, it was a place he felt safe from the pressures of the world.

It was Maud's Garden, she'd designed, planted and lovingly tended the flowers and small vegetable patch right up to her death nearly seven years ago. Although, it was Bob who did the work in the last few months, while she would sit on the veranda and watch, as the cancer devastated her frail body.

He wasn't a gardener but year after year, he weeded, mowed, planted boarders and vegetables. It was his way of keeping her in his life, her memory brought beauty and joy to everyone who passed the house. Her special joy was to create a Christmas Garden and, in her memory, he would make a special show of flowers for Christmas out the front. He needed to get onto this immediately otherwise they wouldn't flower at the right time.

"What will I do?" he said aloud to the beans that were growing up the trellis. No flowers yet, but at least the slugs hadn't got to them. "I should have a plan by now!" His eyebrows knotted together as he looked at the grass, it needed another mow, "Already?" he sighed.

"Spring, and everything's blooming and growing. But mowing lawns every week is not my idea of fun." He was sure he heard Maud's chuckle as the wind swept through the trees at the back of the section.

Walking around the garden beds to the front of the house, he noticed the roses starting to bud, a couple of the miniatures had blooms, they were small and delicate like a picture.

What was the theme he used last year? He shook his head as if trying to remove cobwebs. He'd spent a lot of time on it at the start, and he pursed his lips together as he thought.

No. He shook his head. He couldn't remember and he didn't have time to waste. He had to think what the theme could be this year.

He strolled across the section examining the plants, mostly dead now, that created the boarder along the front of the house, and then to the fence. Here he inspected the perennials scattered between the roses, they'd also had seen better days. When had he last weeded out the front? It must have been some time ago; his mind was a blank. While he'd been incapacitated, the Village Association and a couple of his other organisations had organised a roster to mow the lawn and weed. He'd appreciated it, and it became one less thing to worry about while he had been stuck in hospital. Moving automatically around the garden he struggled to find any inspiration.

"Maud, what do you think? What will we do for Christmas this year?" he asked aloud, "What would you like to see?"

He waited, and walked, and waited some more. But the creativity he'd felt in the past didn't come, and try as he might, he just couldn't feel the joy of the season around him.

"Hello," called a small voice, "what are you doing? Are you gardening?"

The voice had penetrated his concentration and he looked in the direction it came from. It belonged to a young, blonde-haired girl in a pink T-shirt and jeans, peering over the fence, her eyes darting around the garden and then back at him.

This would have been the sixth time this week she'd wandered along the street looking at all the gardens, often just standing on the grass verge, taking in the colourful sights of the flower gardens of Roberts Street.

She stood looking at him, her eyes wide and alert, he could tell she was desperate to say more than just hello. It was just a matter of time.

"Do you like gardening?" she asked politely.

"I guess so." Bob shrugged in her direction then turned to look at another patch of the garden so that his back was almost to her. He wasn't feeling sociable, today he wanted to keep himself to himself and be left alone.

A small seven-year-old voice broke his train of thought. He should have known it wouldn't last.

"My name 's Nicki, but my Mum calls me her Busy Bee!" she said with a beaming smile.

With a quick glance in her direction, he nodded and gave an attempt at a smile. He was about to turn back to the quandary of what to do with the boarders when he caught the disconcerted look on the young face as she waited for the inevitable 'Oh? Why's that, then?' which usually followed her statement. There was just the faintest faltering of her lovely smile and then it was back again.

If Maud had been alive, she'd have answered her properly and no doubt would have brought out a glass of juice for her. She might even have fetched Aggie and Diane's old dolls from the cupboard and let her play with them in the garden. She was always so good at socialising, especially when it came to children. Instead, Nicki gave a cheery wave and wandered off.

Over the following week, the sunny weather continued, Bob brought all his garden books outside to walk along the borders, looking for inspiration.

All the online examples looked like a lot of hard work, he wanted something simple but effective. And each afternoon the small cheerful face continued to appear to appear, always with the smiling 'Hello'. Every day, Nicki would share some interesting event or observation with Bob who would politely reply with the bare minimum of conversation. Some days he enjoyed listening, others he wished Mags would appear and chase the child away.

"There was a fire drill at my school today, and we all got to look at the fire engines, and then go home early," said Nicki the following Friday. "It's going to be summer holidays and then I might get to stay with Mum," Bob's eyebrow raised.

"You don't live with your mother?"

She shook her head, "She's in a special home, to make her better," said the child still smiling, "when she's better, we'll be able to go home."

"Are you staying with Mrs Sykes?" asked Bob, knowing his Village Association secretary was a foster carer. Nicki nodded.

A sudden pang of guilt washed over Bob. He hadn't realised she was in foster care; poor little mite was probably used to being neglected and ignored. That would explain why the child was trying to form some kind of bond with him. He decided to be friendlier, it couldn't be easy for her, at such a young age.

"Where is home?" asked Bob, looking at the child in a new light.

"We had a house in Masterton but I can't live there anymore cause Mum went into hospital and there was no one to look after me. And now Dad lives there and another lady and her boys. They are all older than me and I was supposed to be with him, but the boys …"

Nicki stopped talking and looked down at the ground. Bob could see her smile was gone and she was shaking.

Walking briskly over to her, he stopped by the fence and kneeled down so he was at her height.

"Nicki," he said gently, "you don't have to tell me anything. I guess it just didn't work out, and now you are staying with Mrs Sykes." The child nodded and looked up at Bob, her pale green eyes glistened with tears, as her lower lip trembled.

"Do you like it at Mrs Sykes house?" he asked. She nodded and there was a flicker of a smile. "She has a cat and …" but before Bob could finish, Nicki had found her voice again and told him about the rescued animals that Mrs Sykes had in the Animal rescue shed and what you have to do to nurse them back to health.

"But there is no garden there," said Nicki eventually. "I love gardens, and Mum and I used to do gardening all the time. We would pick the flowers and put them in vases and they would make the house pretty and smelly. It would make Mum smile, especially when she got sick." Nicki gave Bob a sideways look and took a deep sigh.

A warbler called from a tree in the back and a little breeze travelled around the garden rousing the leaves and buds into a happy dance.

It came to him as a spur of the moment decision. Bob asked Nicki if she would like to help him pick out the Christmas flowers for the boarders. The look on her face was of sheer delight and he told her he would arrange it with Mrs Sykes. Nicki headed back to her temporary home with the biggest smile, skipping all the way.

A plan formed in Bob's head, he wondered if any of the other children in care would be interested in gardening, or even baking. This was the turning point, Bob was certain he had found a spark of Christmas spirit, and as the warbler sang its song, he went inside to arrange it with Molly Sykes.

***

The following weekend, Nicki, Louise, an artistic teen in foster care and Molly Sykes showed up at Bob's bright and early at 9.30 on the Saturday morning. Nicki was clutching three large hard covered books that looked way too heavy for her. Lou held one and carried a back pack as Molly ushered them into Bob's kitchen.

Laying the books out on the table, Molly explained they had been busy in the library searching for the right books to help with the Christmas Garden project. Nicki had been studying the plants, helped by Lou who drew them and coloured them to see what would look good together, and where.

"It's for people to have a happy Christmas isn't it Mr Fletcher?" asked Nicki. Bob nodded and leaned over to look at the pencil drawings of the front of his house with the boarders all in full bloom showing a wonderful display of purple, gold and blue flowers along the front, and green and silver foliage plants along the fence line.

"I just copied what was in the books," said Lou as Bob looked astounded at the expert illustrations coloured with pencils. "I selected the colours," she said laughing, "Nicki wanted ALL the colours."

"But we have to leave some out for next year, don't we," explained Nicki. Bob chuckled; he'd never seen anyone so enthusiastic about his garden as these two.

"Young Nicki has already done quite a bit of research," said Molly, "after we explained you needed plants that grew and flowered in summer, needed partial shade because the sun moved, and only a little bit of looking after, she had her nose in those books every day after school till bed time." Nicki's bright infectious smile filled the room and he found himself looking forward to getting the project started.

"First we have to make some cookies for the Saturday Stick Chicks knitting group, I'll be in big trouble if I don't show up with something tasty." said Bob. Lou smiled, she had just started attending the group and she understood.

"What are we going to make?" asked Nicki, a tad reluctant to take her mind off the gardening.

"Flower cookies, two types, one lemon and vanilla and one raspberry and chocolate. I think I need help cutting out the dough." He handed Nicki and Lou each a flower cookie cutter, and then went to the fridge to take out the cookie dough he'd made earlier and left chilling.

With three trays of the cookies in the oven and the timer on, Bob took a good look at the plants they would need to get from a local nursery. On his computer, he checked the nursery stock on their websites and between the three of them, they should be able to get all the plants they needed.

After talking the cookies from the oven, while waiting for them to cool, they ordered the plants online. All that was left was to drive to Clareville and Masterton to pick them up. He'd do that tomorrow. Nicki tried hard, but her smile was fading.

"What's the matter?' Bob asked. "We have the plants ordered, but you don't look very happy."

"I thought we'd get them all today and put them in the ground and then they'd grow and we'd have flowers."

Bob let out a guffaw. "It takes time. First, we have to prepare the ground, and then plant them in the right order. The plants will take a few weeks to grow, and we want the flowers to all bloom when it's Christmas time. We have work to do before we can start."

Nicki's mouth formed an O and her eyes went wide, she pursed her lips together and clenched her fists. He could see she was desperate to get stuck into the gardening.

"We need to pull the old plants out first," said Bob. So, while these cookies cool, we'll start on that, ok?" Her face lit up and all four of them went out to Bob's gardening shed to collect the tools they'd need to prepare the flower beds.

Both Nicki and Lou were kneeing on the gardening cushions, each wearing a pair of Maud's old gardening gloves and Nicki had Maud's straw hat shading her fair skin. They carefully pulled out plants and weeds as Bob instructed. Remembering back to the time Nicki chatted to him over the fence, he recalled her mother's nickname for the livewire was Busy Bee. She certainly was, he mused, as he joined Molly on the verandah.

"I know I'm not supposed to know about their circumstances, but Nicki said her mother was sick and was in a home. I'd like to give Nicki some flowers to take to her when she visits if that is alright." Bob just blurted out. Approaching these sensitive subjects delicately was not a strong point for him, he preferred getting straight to the point.

Molly Sykes took a sip of her lemonade and contemplated how much information she should pass on to Bob. Looking out at the road, she quickly reviewed Nicki's situation.

It was a warm day and Molly was pleased she'd worn her cotton sun frock, as condensation from her glass dripped onto the skirt.

Placing the glass back on the table she turned to Bob. Her eyes searched his face, she'd known him a long time and decided that he had both integrity and empathy enough to hear Pam's story. She chose her words carefully as she explained that Pam had fallen for a charismatic and older man, who had swept her off her feet. She was young and impressionable and in love, and then pregnant. She moved in with him, but he seemed to be more interested in building his business, and then Nicki was born.

"Her father dotted on her from all accounts, but when Nicki was turned six, something went wrong with his business. He tried to sell the house they lived in to get money, but he'd put it in Pam's name to avoid tax." Molly took a sip of her lemonade, "Well, long story short. He was still married and his wife turned up one day and there was a fight, kicked her out not knowing there was a child." Bob nodded. 'These things happen,' he thought

"A court case and custody battle for Nicki took its toll on Pam's health. She was only twenty-five and there was no one in her corner to help. Then after intimidation from the wife and the teenage sons; she had a turn. They think was a stroke. It's thought she was attacked, hit in the head, but she fell and they couldn't decide if it was from the fall or not. Nicki's father told them not to pursue further investigation into what caused it." Molly looked out at the garden her eyes narrowed and her jaw clenched. Bob could see she was angry about the decision.

"Anyway, the result is that she's been in a coma ever since, and is in a long-term care facility. Nicki was put in her father's custody but that didn't work out, and now she's with me. We try to see her mother once a month, and it just breaks my heart to see the child chattering away to her unconscious mother, telling her all the things she's been doing and, well, no one really knows when Pam will wake up, if ever."

The silence between them was amicable as each thought about the circumstances that had been affecting Nicki for almost six months. Bob bit his bottom lip, and felt slightly ashamed that he'd thought of Nicki as a neglected child. Just goes to show, not all kids in care are abused, some have just had a raw deal, and he was annoyed he had assumed. His admiration for Nicki increased, she had a lot to put up with but still she managed to look at the bright side of life.

"Not just flowers then," said Bob, "a pot plant, one that doesn't take much care, but Nicki can tend to it when she visits."

He believed he knew what was needed. With that he stood up and went to check on the gardening. It was time to stop and decorate the cookies ready for the Stick Chicks knitting group.

Sir Neville Emerson

"Good morning, Sarah, and what a beautiful morning it is. A promise of a long hot summer to come I think."

Sir Neville Emerson was standing in the French doors leading out onto the concrete patio. His back was to Sarah, who placed the folder she was carrying on his desk and went to join him.

"You're in a good mood this morning," said Sarah, a single eyebrow raised. The last week had been difficult. As Sarah's wife would say, 'there'd been trouble at t'mill'. And Sir Neville was annoyed that he had to go in to the office and sort out the mess. He hated letting people go, but when they have been proven to be working against him and the businesses, he had spent a lifetime building, there was no choice.

"I signed the last of the papers last night and now it's all up to you and the lawyers. I've finished. I don't want to hear any more about it. OK?" he turned and looked at his personal assistant.

As usual her dark hair was pulled into a severe bun at the base of her neck, and today's practical clothes were a dark blue skirt and cream coloured blouse, always the professional, in her smart business clothes. A wave of pride rose in his chest, he pursed his lips together and looked out at the view.

The lawn, the yew hedge behind the two shade trees, all in shimmering shades of green. As spring awoke the sleeping buds of the trees, the leaves were putting on a show covering the once naked skeleton, now bursting with greenery.

With a curt nod of her head, Sarah moved back to her desk at the side of the room. She opened a desk diary at today's date and ran her finger down the list of things to do and appointments for the day. She looked at her watch, it was ten minutes past eight. The first meeting of the day was at nine, in Thornbury.

"Do you want me to come to the meeting at the Hog and Frog at nine?" she asked.

"Eh?" replied Sir Neville, still engrossed in the glorious late spring morning.

"The meeting at nine, should I be there to take notes?"

Turning back into the room, like a naughty schoolboy caught skiving off, he nodded.

"It's a planning meeting, or at least that's what I called it. Mark and Mandy may have other things to discuss, but I'm looking at the usual Christmas party for the Grandparents Raising Grandchildren crowd and the Foster Carers in the area, and the Christmas Day lunch. Goodness knows those groups need all the help they can get at this time of the year.

We'll give them a good day, and I've got some ideas already. Take a note. First, we will bus them all out here, have a Christmas treasure hunt for treats, barbeque lunch and games, face painting, bouncy castle and all that. I'll leave that up to you and our event planner. Then back into town and home.

That will be the Saturday. Then alternatively on Sunday afternoon games and early evening Christmas dinner in the town hall with all the works, Santa and presents. You know how much I enjoy dressing up at Christmas." Sarah chuckled; he was like a kid in a candy store at this time of year. "Or we could have the whole weekend before Christmas, put everyone in good spirits. Oh, we need to get numbers and any special diets of course. All the usual." Sir Neville stopped talking and took a big sigh. "There will be some who will need a little bit of help at home as well. I'll let you and the party planner find out who needs what, on the quiet of course."

"Of course," replied Sarah. This was the usual drill, no one was to know that the set of Christmas lights or decorations or food hamper that turned up on the front door with two months' worth of power paid, came from Sir Neville, but from an anonymous donor. His job was being Santa and handing out the presents, he and his wife had lost their only child years ago in an accident, and he had consoled himself by taking on charity work for children. He had tried to involve his wife, but she felt he was being unfaithful to the memory of their son, and slowly they had drifted apart until her premature death of an evasive cancer.

Instead of wallowing, he took on more charity work, and the children, carers and medical staff at the local hospitals and hospices on Christmas eve and the lunch for Thornbury locals who were alone on Christmas Day.

'If you're a multi-millionaire,' thought Sarah, 'this is exactly what you should do with all that money. Give back to your community.'

The ethics of the Emerson Corporation and her boss Sir Neville sat well with her beliefs, she couldn't have wanted a better job or boss.

"The new woman would do that," continued Sir Neville as Sarah brought herself back to the present. "What was her name again?"

"Rhonda, her name is Rhonda Barry."

He thanked her, again he felt a welling of pride, but now was not the time. "To the auto-mobile!" he said, and Sarah giggled. Sir Neville stood with his feet slightly apart. One arm raised and the other on his hip, looking just like the Batman character from the 1960's television show.

Grabbing her bag, and suit jacket, she followed him out to the car and the first appointment of the day.

Mark and Mandy Weatherby

Mark Weatherby held open the door for his wife who nodded thanks as she walked through into the cool darkness of the Hog and Frog bar. Mandy took off her sunglasses, the contrast from the bright light outdoors to the dark wood of the hundred-year-old pub was stark. Looking around she saw their regulars, the group of retired men who meet every afternoon after lunch for a 'constitutional', to reminisce about the old times and to play a game of cards.

Another small group were huddled together near a corner, eyes firmly fixed on pieces of paper while one person was reading. 'Could be a business meeting,' she thought, as she recognised a couple of faces from the council, but then noticed the woman that seemed to be in charge. A brief smile crossed her lips, the local amateur theatre, getting ready for their yearly Christmas extravaganza, she decided.

"What can I get you love?" asked Mark, a concerned frown over his face. He was standing behind the bar, looking at his wife. Her short wavy hair was now a sandy brown, her long well filled out face now seemed drawn accentuating her features.

Her shoulders sagged. There was a slight tremble in her hands, and he wanted to reach out and hug her, to take her away from the heartbreak that was so visible on her face.

"I know it's still early, but a light cider would be nice," she said with a smile that didn't reach her blue-grey eyes. "I'll take it up to our rooms. Are you going to stay here?" she asked, a look of anticipation on her face.

"I'll be up in a minute," he said handing her the cold bottle, "just need to check in with everyone, see if they need anything," Mandy nodded, took the bottle and walked to the door leading into the hallway and the back, staff only, staircase.

Mark watched her leave, noticing that the limp on her right foot seemed to be more prominent than usual. He wished there was something he could do to help her, but the news she received last week was a blow, they were still coming to terms with it. It's never a good sign getting bad news the very end of November. It was starting to build up to the busiest time of the year, and their focus should be on making the groups coming in for their pre-Christmas celebrations the best ever. Every year Mark marvelled at the décor and decorations that Mandy arranged, each year with a theme that somehow just made this time of year even more special.

Their meeting that morning with Sir Neville. Rhonda and Sarah had been fun and exciting.

Mandy's face was full of joy as she gave them her ideas for the yearly Christmas party. Even the new event manager was quick to pick up on Mandy's creativity and was happy to go with it. What would happen with it now, he wondered.

He sighed and did a quick check that all was in order behind the bar. It would take a few weeks, but he wondered if Mandy would be able to get involved like she used to. It could be a distraction for her or it could be a hindrance. How Mandy would feel, he just didn't know, and under usual circumstances this would be the week she made all the decisions and started the decorating.

Thankfully Heather, their itinerant summer worker had turned up last week, and he was happy to take her on again, even after the unpleasantness of the last year with the local doctor. He didn't care. There was work to be done, and Heather was a reliable and trustworthy worker.

There was a crash in the kitchen and Mark rushed through into the restaurant to check if anyone was hurt. There was no one around so he made his way into the kitchen. In the middle of the room, staring at a large metal tray lying on the floor, stood Rick, the recently hired kitchen assistant and trainee hotelier.

"I … dropped it," her stammered looking from the tray to Mark and back again.

"I gathered that," replied Mark trying to keep a straight face, "is Chef here?" Rick didn't need to reply, Mark already knew the answer. If Chef had been around, Rick would have been getting a telling off for being clumsy.

The kitchen door opened and Heather rushed in. "What the!" she exclaimed looking at Rick then Mark who pointed at the tray lying on the ground. Heather threw her head back and laughed, a gentle musical lilt that made both men stare at her.

Rick felt his face flush but he couldn't tell if it was in embarrassment of being so foolish in front of Heather, or if it was in fascination of her. He didn't know why, but he found himself rattled every time she was near. Even now he dropped the tray, just because she had walked past the serving counter, and she hadn't even noticed him. His face burned, he had to get a grip! He'd just come back from two years in the army, serving in Afghanistan. He'd dealt with ambushes, snipers, Americans, and the weather. Why was he a blethering idiot around this woman? And what would he do if Bron found out?

Standing with her hands on her slim hips, Heather shook her head. Her light brown hair was tied back in a ponytail, with a face that glowed with good health. Her green eyes sparkled as she laughed. Mark smiled, he knew the affect Heather had on men and he thought of the 29-year-old as a daughter.

"Glad you're here," said Mark, ignoring the flustered Rick. "Mandy's had a rough day so we'll be in the apartment for the evening. Heather, you are in charge. Tina will down soon to do the evening shift in the dining room. We don't have many bookings but I expect there will be some walk-ins." Heather nodded; her face serious. "Come get me if it gets too busy for you and Tina. Chef and Ross will be in the kitchen, they should be here about 4.30 but … if you think Rick's up to it, train him up behind the bar."

It was a throw away remark that caused Rick to gasp and Heather to raise an eyebrow, to look over at Rick and then at the tray still lying on the kitchen floor.

"I can show him the basics," she said, turning back to look at Mark, as if to say, 'are you sure!' Turning back to Rick she smiled. "When the Chef comes in, you come over to the bar, and I'll put you through the paces." He nodded, he was trying to look cool, while his heart pounded and he swallowed back the fear that was rising from his stomach.

"Wonderful. You'll be fine, Rick. Trust what Heather says, she's been with us for four years now, so she knows just as much as I do." With that, he and Heather left the kitchen, leaving Rick to come to terms with working closely with a woman that he now realised he was infatuated with.

Leaving them to it, Mark climbed the stairs to the guest rooms, passing Tina who was the afternoon housekeeper today. He told her the same as the others, that he and Mandy would take it easy, then walked through the staff only door to the back of the hotel and their rooms.

What had been the old servant's quarters in the 1900's hotel had been turned into a cosy lounge with a kitchen/dinner off it on one side, and two bedrooms with a shared bathroom.

When he entered the lounge, he saw Mandy sitting staring at the fireplace on the outside wall. He wondered if she were thinking of ways to decorate it, as she did every Christmas.

The fireplace was a feature on the wall, unused for decades and impractical to repair, they had patched it up and put a standing heat pump in, keeping the facade and mantel piece.

Mandy picked up her phone and handed it to Mark.

"I have an appointment already for radiation therapy," Mark looked down at the phone, in just two days' time and out of the area, of course. But this was important and Mandy was the most important person in his life. He would do what he had to; they would get through this.

"I'll get you there, don't you worry," he said and sat next to her holding her hand. "Heather can be the bar manager and I can get someone in to work on the kitchen and bookings."

"That woman that helps out around the Wellington region, she was good."

"Exactly my thoughts, I just hope no one else had snapped her up."

"Oh, Sir Neville's event," said Mandy, a look of horror on her face, "I can't let him down."

"I think that new event manager he's employed would be happy to help, she seemed nice." Mark smiled but didn't get a return smile from Mandy. She was worrying about others instead of thinking about herself, as usual. "I'll contact her, see what she says," he added. Mandy nodded but didn't smile.

"I expect we should tell John," Mandy sighed.

"Do you want to?" he asked and she shook her head.

"Maybe later when we have more information. I should check if he's coming here for Christmas."

Mandy picked up her phone and sent a text. "I won't expect an answer for a while. He's probably so busy he's forgotten what time of the year it is."

***

Inspector John Dowling was sitting in his car observing a building of interest. He looked down at his phone as the text came in, he decided he'd deal to that after hours, right now he had to check if their informant was right.

This particular group posed as members of a fringe Christian group, but the information they'd received was horrifying. Their lead included documents that indicated they were part of a human trafficking network.

As the inspector and the plainclothes constable watched, a car pulled up outside the warehouse and two men got out. From the back seat a young woman emerged, her hair was short, red-brown in colour, her lipstick was pale but she had dark eye makeup. He guessed her age was probably between 18 and 25, tall and slim. He picked the camera up and zoomed in to take shots. The camera clicked away as he watched the two men usher the young woman into the building.

Inspector Dowling put the camera down and sat back in his seat. That was a surprise. After all the weeks of work on this case, the last thing he had expected to see was a face he recognised from Thornbury, somewhat different from the last time he'd seen her, but without a doubt, a young woman who was known to them.

*"A real friend is one who walks in when the rest of
the world walks out."*

– Walter Winchell

December- the first week

Molly Sykes and Louise

Molly Sykes paced up and down the station platform, then stopped to look at her watch. She gave an exasperated sigh and pulled at the neck of her cotton dress; it was sticking to her this humid afternoon. She checked her phone again, no texts, no messages, no missed calls; her forehead furrowed into an agonized frown. She had sent multiple texts; all calls had gone directly to voicemail and she was trying not to worry. All along she'd been telling herself it was alright, there would be a perfectly good explanation and dealing with teenagers was always full of difficulties. They don't mean to be inconsiderate, often it is just because they don't think.

She went to send another text and stopped. They could still be in the tunnel, and there's no cell signal, but she was finding it increasingly difficult to be patient.

Louise was supposed to arrive back last night but had sent a text earlier in the day saying she would stay with friends. They wanted to go out to dinner and celebrate. Molly knew her 18-year-old foster child needed to be with friends, she'd had so few people on her side most of her life. It made her happy to think she was starting to live.

Moving into the shade of the small wooden hut that was used as a shelter on rainy days, Molly thought back to the events of just three days ago.

It had been an anxious day, the Wairarapa commuter trains had a reputation of being late or breaking down and this was the time they were relying on them.

For Louise, it was final exam week and a trip into Wellington had to allow for plenty of time to get to Mt. Cook so she could sit the first of her final exams. Molly Sykes had been beyond worried, what would happen if she didn't make the appointment on time?

But Molly need not have worried, it had been their lucky day, with the train arriving on time and Louise had sent a text to say she was at the tech with half hour to spare.

With two days and one morning of exams, they had arranged for Louise to stay in Wellington for two nights with a friend of Molly's rather than return to Thornbury and risk a daily train commute. Doing fabric design and hairdressing meant there were written exams and practical, and Molly remembered the anxiety they both had as Lou took off for Wellington just two days ago.

A train whistle brought Molly out of her thoughts. There was a collective cheer from the various parents and family members waiting for the passengers along the platform. A group of parents with young children stood by the edge of the platform. End of year summer camp for the local primary school Molly thought as she recognised some of the Year seven and eight parents in the crowd.

For many secondary and tertiary students, it was end of term and they were finished for the year. Students were leaving their hostels and boarding arrangements to return home for the holidays, and Molly recognised some of those parents waiting patiently.

A glance at the phone in her hand showed her the train was over 30 minutes late.

Thursday and last of the tech exams for Lou. Molly had filled the time waiting for the train by chatting with a few of the anxious parents along the platform. They all shared their anxious yet familiar stories. It didn't matter how much you nagged and encouraged, had their teens done enough to pass? It was too late to worry about it now and all they could hope there had been enough assignments completed and enough study done.

The sound of an engine caused heads to turn toward the south, and as it drew closer several younger siblings were leaning precariously over the edge of the tracks hoping for a glimpse of the train as it turned the corner into view.

"It's here, it's here ..." the call started with one child and echoed around the platform as the other children picked up the cry. Car doors banged as people got out of their cars and moving forward onto the platform. It was an agonising five minutes before the train had slowed to a stop and started releasing over heated, frazzled and weary eyed students, commuters, and a few holiday makers. Molly, being of average height, couldn't see over the throng, even standing on tiptoe all that spread before her was the tops of heads.

Over the chatter and chaos of shouts and squeals, doors slammed and engines revved as cars jockeyed for position, trying to avoid a traffic jam on their way out of the 'park and ride' area. Regular daily commuters walked down the streets to their homes and as the crowd thinned out Molly looked anxiously for Lou.

She was looking for the tall slim 18-year-old, probably dressed in black ripped jeans, a black t-shirt, with goth makeup, long hair parted in the middle and dyed in a colour combination of dark green and mauve over black. At least that was the goth look Molly remembered, it could be anything now after 3 days away.

A few late pick-ups arrived and Molly saw two men in long trench coats, walking along the platform toward the back end of the train, while peering in the windows of the train carriages. The day was a real scorcher and anyone in a coat like that would have been extremely hot. It immediately made the heckles on her neck rise, she instinctively felt they were trouble.

As someone jumped out of a doorway onto the platform and started moving toward the centre of the station. The two trench coats got to the end and then turned to look back at the crowd. They were tall, and soon spotted their prey, running toward the person who was now moving quickly down the platform dodging people as they went. Molly could see them all getting closer, but she still didn't recognise any of them.

With a sudden whoosh, the train slowly started to move along the track, building speed as it prepared to leave the station with a grand blast of the whistle.

There were people milling around, waiting for the bus connection, others were having reunions or sorting out luggage, taking photos, talking on phones. The two men seemed to have now caught up with their quarry.

A car roared into the park and ride, and Molly frowned.

'That's not on. They should drive carefully with so many people about,' she thought, 'even if they are running late.'

It was an agonising minute or so as Molly searched through the people still on the platform No-one took any notice her, until she came to the two inappropriately dressed men. They were arguing with the third person who had tried to elude them. One man was trying to grab her arm but she kept pushing them away and kicking out at them and had her back to Molly. The young woman was tall and slim, like Lou, but her reddish-brown hair was cut short, and hugged her head, she wore a floral short sleeved dress. Molly had never seen Lou in anything floral, and definitely never in a dress.

This was not the time to be side tracked by clothes, thought Molly. The behaviour of the two men was unacceptable, and even though the woman probably wasn't Lou at all, there was something familiar about her. Taking a deep breath she waded into them, grabbing the young woman away and standing between her and the two men.

"Get out of the way!" said one of the men in a deep voice.

"This has nothing to do with you!" snarled the other who raised his arm to push Molly out of the way. A sudden scream echoed around the station and the young woman ran off down the steps into the park and ride.

"Stop her!" yelled one of the men, pushing Molly with excessive force as several people turned to look. Molly crashed to the ground, scaping the skin from her knee.

The young woman had run straight into another man who was holding her and calling to another who was talking to her. Molly's blood ran cold, how many men were after this woman?

She didn't care what she'd done, no one should be treated like that. She tried to stand up and got to her knees when she saw one of the men coming straight for her. She braced herself for a sudden impact and was ready to pull him to the ground with her.

"Help me, please Mrs Sykes, they're taking me away," the young woman was calling to her and Molly looked up again to see her staring in her direction. With pounding heart Molly took a deep breath, she needed to steady herself, the man was nearly by her side. She looked over to the young woman again. She was staring at her intently. Slowly it dawned on her and she gave a small yelp.

"Louise!" The young woman's face seemed to relax just a little now she was recognised, even though it was still screwed up in fear.

An arm reached out and clutched Molly's shoulder, she grabbed the wrist with her other hand and gave a sharp pull, causing the man to lose balance and crash to the ground beside her. She looked over at him, her hand balled to a fist, ready to defend herself when she noticed the man was laughing. She looked closely at his face and was horrified to see it was Officer Jamie. Her face felt hot, as she wondered how she would justify taking out the local police officer.

"Well done Mrs Sykes," said Officer Jamie still amused that his middle-aged pupil had managed to best him.

"Oh, I'm so sorry," she replied in a hushed tone, "I didn't know it was you."

"That's ok," said the police constable, he stood up then put his hand out to help Molly up. "I'm pleased you kept you head and defended yourself. You're my star pupil now." Swallowing hard, Molly was surprised he wasn't angry with her.

"Are you hurt?" she asked, fearful that there could be repercussions as a foster carer.

"The under 7's rugby team causes more damage than that to me every Saturday," he added, "but I think there is someone here who needs your help." He pointed over toward Lou. "Inspector Dowling is looking after her for now, but you need to get down there."

"Lou, I'm coming," she called out and headed toward the group with a sense of dread.

"Hey!" she called out, quickly clasping Louise's arm as one of the two men tried to drag the teen away. The other man had punched Inspector Dowling, who was now defending himself.

"What are you doing?" called out Molly, mustering as much courage as she could. She could see people on the platform taking notice now, and she recognised a couple of them from the Village Association.

"Get lost lady," said the man continuing to drag Lou away. "This is none of your business."

"It is my business," she said pulling herself up to her full height. She felt her initial feeling of shock become rapidly replaced with anger. No one tells her what to do when it came to the safety of the children in her care. She glared at the two men, above average height, with non-descript faces, short hair, and bland features. They were both dressed the same and if it hadn't been for the trench coats, she might not have looked at them twice.

"How is that?" asked the man, taking a step toward her. 'He's trying to intimidate me', she thought.

"This young woman is in my care; I'm her guardian. Where do you think you are taking her?" Molly kept her voice steady as she tried to remember everything she'd learnt from the 'keep yourself safe' courses for carers with the welfare association and that nice Constable McKay in Masterton. Officer Jamie helped Inspector Dowling up off the ground, while keeping an eye on the men.

"That's BS, she's a runaway and we're taking her home to her parents. We have all the right paperwork from the court. So, get lost!" The man was only two steps away from Molly, she could feel her heart pounding, as she tried to suppress the desire to run. Her brows wrinkled, and she gritted her teeth, ready for a fight.

"I don't want to go home," cried Louise, "you can't make me, they threw me out!"

"Liar!" said the other man as he turned away from Inspector Dowling. A mistake as the inspector had him on the ground and handcuffed before he knew what had happened.

The other man stepped in front of Louise, his face barely a hand width from her face.

"We know you make up stories and drag other people into your lies. You seem unable to face the truth, and your belief that your lies are true means you're a danger to everyone around you. We're here to protect you and help you." Lou tried to step away from the man who was in her face. He grabbed her shoulder.

"The pastor and your parents will cure you of your sin of bearing false witness." Lou sobbed, she looked over at Molly, a tear trickle down her face. The young woman's face was screwed up in fear as she shook her head. She was breathing rapidly.

"That is not a lie, please believe me," she said. That was when Molly lost her temper.

"How dare you!" she screamed at the man in front of Lou, he looked startled as he turned to look at her. "I was the one who got the phone call at midnight asking if she could stay with me. Her parents had packed her bags and put them outside, locked the door and wouldn't let her in. You have no idea what this young woman has been through and now that she's safe, all you want to do is take it away from her. You should be ashamed of yourselves." She looked at the man in front of her who showed no emotion and the handcuffed man that Officer Jamie was about to escort to the car.

"Call yourself Christians?" she asked, "I'm sure Jesus didn't use intimidation and brute force to get his followers, he did it with love and understanding. Two traits that you seem to be totally void of. If you think you can kidnap my foster daughter, you have another thing coming." Molly Sykes looked over at the inspector and Officer Jamie. They both stood there, eyes wide as they watched the middle-aged woman take on the would-be kidnapper.

"They don't know who they are messing with, do they Inspector Dowling and Officer Jamie?" Molly said their names slowly, pleased to see a baffled look cross the face of the men.

She didn't know why either of them happened to be at the railway station right there and then, but someone or something was looking after Lou, and that was fine by her. The girl needed someone on her side and if that was divine intervention, then it was about time.

Officer Jamie quickly handcuffed the second man, and as they were taken away, Molly hugged Lou who sobbed then blurted out her thanks over and over.

While Officer Jamie guarded the two men in the back of the unmarked police car, the inspector helped Molly to calm Lou. She then told of how they had lured her away by saying her brothers and sisters wanted to see her in secret. She recognised the men who had sometimes been at their church. It was the only reason she went with them.

"I feel like such a fool. I'm so sorry," said Lou wiping her face with the back of her hand. "I thought it would be nice to see my family, but they weren't there. They'd tricked me and kept asking me questions about what my family was doing and when would I see them again and it was the same questions over and over."

"Come and sit in the car, you look exhausted," said Molly, guiding Lou over to her car after Inspector Dowling and Officer Jamie had arranged for her to give a statement at the police station the next day.

It took a couple of minutes for the cool air to come through the air conditioner and take the heat out of the car which had been sitting in the sun for almost an hour. As the temperature lowered, Lou started to relax, even though she was still trembling.

"They wouldn't let me sleep or eat, and when they gave me food it tasted funny so I wouldn't eat it. It made them angry and they tried to force it in my mouth." Lou shuddered at the memory. "I kicked one of them," she said.

"Did you? They must have really upset you." Lou nodded, and the edge of her mouth curled sightly. Molly looked at the teen in front of her who looked so different from the last time she'd seen her.

"He went to slap me but the other man stopped him. He said something funny, like, we don't want to damage the goods, or something like that." This made Molly raise an eyebrow as she looked at Lou, it was an odd thing to say.

"It was dark, and they wouldn't let me sleep, they keep asking questions and then they'd leave me for about half an hour, I'd lean on the table and close my eyes but every time I thought I'd just be ready to fall asleep, they'd come in and wake me and start with the questions again." She took a deep breath. "It was a very long night."

"I have to ask," said Molly, "but why did you cut your hair and change colour?"

"Oh, well part of it was the exam." Molly gasped, in all the excitement she'd forgotten to ask how the exams and assessments went. Lou smiled. "I was one of the models, for one of the second years, they had to do a complete colour change. She did a great job, cause getting rid of black is hard and I toned down my make up just a bit for the assessment. Then I had a first year trim my hair, it wasn't supposed to be this short, I think she was so nervous she made a mistake and then had to keep going. I'm sure she did enough to pass."

"I bet you were surprised when you saw it, but it looks wonderful," said Molly smiling.

A red tinge rose in Lou's pale cheeks, she still found it very uncomfortable to accept a complement, even with Molly's patient confidence building going on. "But how did those men know it was you?

"I thought about that, I guess it was the heavy make-up and the goth clothes, but we were all calling out to each other in the streets, talking about meeting up and I think they were there, outside the tech. They would have heard people calling my name."

'That would explain it' thought Molly, 'just bad luck.'

"It must have been around dawn when they made me change clothes into this dress, then wash off my makeup. I wouldn't do it, but then they started being nice and said they'd give me an apple and a chocolate bar if I did." Tears welled in her eyes again and Molly reached over and took her hand. "I was just so hungry, and I didn't think it would hurt."

"That's ok," added Molly to reassure her.

"But they didn't give me anything, they put me in the car and then we drove away."

"How ever did you get away?" Molly was intrigued.

"We were in Wellington, in the city and the car stopped for a traffic light. I bolted, and they couldn't turn or pull over because there was a bus behind them and no parking. It's all one-way streets too, so I ran. I guess they worked out I'd try and get on the Wairarapa train." Lou took a breath; she was feeling more distressed that she let on and reliving the ordeal was upsetting. Even on this hot summer day, she felt cold.

"I saw them at the station waiting for the morning train so I hid until the one that had the most people on it. I thought I'd got away with it, but then I saw them searching the carriages and I panicked. I was sure they'd catch me before we arrived in Thornbury."

"But Lou, how did you get a ticket?" So far everything had been believable Molly wondered how she managed to evade the train guards. Lou gave a weak smile and put her hand down the front of her dress, pulling out a bank card holder made of fabric on a thin piece of ribbon.

"It was a mini project in textiles, keeping ourselves safe. Keep your bank card and some cash or other important things hidden in your bra. Well, for the women that is." Molly chuckled, yes, she knew that trick.

"Oh, well done Louise, well done."

A couple of cars left the carpark, and Molly pulled her seat-belt on. "Time to get you some rest and food, plus the others will be wanting to know how your exams went. I'm surprised they haven't sent you texts already."

Pulling her seatbelt down, Lou looked out the front of the car, "They took my phone," she said quietly.

As they drove out of the park and ride, Molly wondered how she'd be able to afford to get a new phone for Louise. The young woman deserved a break and with Christmas just a couple of weeks away, what a perfect time to surprise her.

Driving down the street Molly looked at the decorative banners that were going up on the street lamps and remembered Sir Neville and his generous Christmas parties.

That was it, she'd contact him and see if he could help. But what if he said 'No'. It was no time for doubt, it was the season for good will and Molly decided to keep a positive frame of mind for Lou's sake. It didn't matter if you were eighteen or eight, no one should have to go through an ordeal like that, especially at this time of year.

Nettie Sanderson

The last Christmas card was tucked neatly into its envelope and Nettie sat back in her chair, looking at the small pile of cards in front of her. Each year she contemplated the pile of envelopes and thought of the names of friends and family who were no longer.

It was a dull Sunday morning, drizzly and humid, almost like being in a tropical hot house. Prissy mewed at the closed deck door, expecting to be let out.

"You won't like being outside," said Nettie to the petite black and white cat, "you're a bit of a hot house plant, you don't like the rain." Prissy turned and looked at Nettie with such disdain, that she ended up opening the door. It wasn't the first time Nettie was sure Prissy understood everything she said.

As if to prove she didn't care what the weather was doing, Prissy waked out onto the wet deck and sat down. Nettie shrugged and was about to close the door when a black and white streak rushed past her leaving big wet paw prints over the kitchen floor.

"Told you," said Nettie with a smile.

The clock by the stove showed it was just after nine, and this morning she needed to get ready to join Bron at the shop.

Mel was still away after her terrible accident and this was a busy time of year, not so much for the purchasing of wool, but for the wool crafts and products that she also sold at Nettie's Knit Shop in the village.

Amber-May's bespoke knits and patterns were selling well, but her teen-aged daughter, Sacha-Rose had created a lovely range of knitted and felted Christmas decorations, so unique and colourful that they were becoming the shop's best-selling item. Even Mags, the shop manager, had got into the Christmas spirit with a selection of knitted summer tops in cotton blends that was just the epitome of summer.

The shop had been decorated, Mags, Amber-May and Sacha-Rose had taken over one afternoon, and Nettie was pleased they did, they had more creativity for displays in their little fingers than she did in her whole body.

Finishing off her coffee before heading to the shower, Nettie wished she felt more Christmassy but the phone call last evening to her daughter had taken that all away.

It had been difficult to listen to Vanessa enthusiastically talking about her plans to go tramping with friends in Fiordland National Park. She'd be with her university friends, a great group who were always lively and doing good deeds in their spare time. This year they were making an adventure of it, using the summer break to work with the Department of Conservation for bird counting and tagging on some of the tiny remote islands around the mainland. It was a great opportunity for Vanessa, Nettie had to admit, as she tried to hide her disappointment.

Her son Ryan, Hannah and six-year-old Greena were spending the season with Hannah's family, and it sounded like such a lovely holiday for them on Waiheke Island for a week. She was happy for them all, but disappointed she wouldn't see them until the new year.

This would be the first year that neither Vanessa nor Ryan and his family would be spending Christmas with her. It was just her and Prissy, and she wouldn't be surprised if Prissy had plans as well. She was just as comfortable next door at Sam's house, keeping company with Lulu the partially blind chihuahua.

Looking down at the address on the card that sat on top of the pile brought a smile to Nettie. It was to her dear friend and once neighbour, Beth. Picking up the envelope, she took the card out and added a long note to the bottom. She'd been neglectful as a friend, caught up in village life and running the shop. Now was a perfect time to rekindle their friendship and what better way than inviting her to stay for Christmas.

With a lighter heart, Nettie readied herself for the shop, and even though it was damp and muggy, she decided to walk. She needed the exercise to walk off the too many fruit-mince pies and chocolate Santa's that would be devoured over the next few weeks.

By the time she arrived at the shops in The Mews, the rain had stopped and a light breeze coming off the Tararua Ranges was starting to blow the low clouds away. It would turn out to be a bright clear day after all.

From the moment the doors were opened there was a constant stream of customers. Many from over the hill, Wellington weekenders looking for something unique and quaint for presents.

Bron and Nettie were kept busy all day, but Nettie found the day full of fun. Around lunchtime, Mags popped in with more stock, and Nettie sent Bron off to the Yellow Strawberry café two shops over, to bring back some sweet cake treats while she put the kettle on.

Mags stood by the doorway between the kitchen and the shop watching out for customers while Nettie made a plunger of coffee and got three mugs out of the cupboard. The back door opened and Bron arrived with a selection of new Christmas treats from the café for them to try.

"I think Mags wants to talk to you," whispered Bron, "I'll look after the shop while you have a break. Draw the quilt over the door, then you'll have some privacy."

'How had I missed that?' thought Nettie, as she turned to look at her friend. Once they were sitting at the table, Nettie realised that Mags wasn't her old self, and just how jumpy she had become.

"Penny for them," said Nettie dropping a couple of saccharin tablets in her mug.

"Eh?" Mags jumped when Nettie stirred her coffee, something was definitely up, Mags was distracted. taking the mug Nettie handed her, Mags sat at the kitchen table looking down into the liquid. Nettie waited.

"It's Bob!" Mags exclaimed; Nettie raised her eyebrow. "He's … he's entertaining. He has visitors." Nettie's eyes opened wide. "The last two weekends he's had a child with him, gardening and I asked him if he wanted to go for a walk last Sunday, but he said he was too busy." Mags turned away and sniffed.

"I, … and I don't even know where the child comes from. He doesn't have any grandchildren around here. I think it's one of those foster kids that Molly Sykes looks after."

"They are gardening? Why would he have a child working in the garden?" Nettie was intrigued.

She knew Bob had a lovely Christmas display in his garden last year. Was this something he did every year? She hadn't been in the village long enough to know.

"Oh, what do I know!" said Mags, pouting.

"He mentioned that the Christmas Garden was going to be a surprise this year both knitting groups," said Nettie, "I heard Rita and a couple of the others trying to get details but he was very tight lipped about it. All he'd say was he had a secret helper so it would be the best ever."

"Hump," responded Mags, "That's supposed to be me! I helped him last year with his Christmas Garden, because of his accident, and I thought we worked really well together. And now … he didn't even think about asking me this year, he just went ahead and now has that child helping!"

"Did you ask him about it?" asked Nettie then saw the strange look she got back and added, "What did he say?"

This was unlike Mags, she suddenly slumped over the kitchen table, her head in her hands and Nettie was sure she was sobbing. Picking up one of the sweet treats from the café, Nettie slowly ate and sipped coffee while waiting for Mags to compose herself. The forty something woman was distressed, known for her explosive outbursts, this was quite different.

"He said he thought I didn't like children, and that this child loved gardening, and that's why he didn't ask me to join them. How could he think I don't like children?" Mags looked at Nettie, her eyes full of tears and her strawberry red hair disheveled.

"I guess he assumed," replied Nettie, "after all, you have no children and we have never seen you around children." Mags sucked in her cheek and looked to the floor.

"Oh, you tell the kids off when they try and ride their bikes through the car park or on the walkway in front of The Mews. They are all pretty scared of you," continued Nettie.

"Oh," said Mags meekly. "I see. I guess that's right, Bob's only seen me disciplining bad behaviour," she said, wiping her hair back from her face.

She took a deep sigh, followed by a gulp of coffee. "I do like kids, I like my nieces and nephews and cousins, but they aren't here, are they?" A frown appeared on her forehead, and she gulped more coffee. "Do you think he'll … I don't know, stop liking me because he thinks I don't get on with kids?"

"To be honest Mags," said Nettie bracing herself, "I wouldn't believe that Bob was particularly fond of kids either, until you told me he was spending time with a child, working in the garden. He's been known to shoo them away and to growl when they are breaking the rules. His kids are grown, and the girls don't have children and they all live far away so ..." Nettie tipped her head to one side and looked up at the ceiling.

"I wonder what it is about that child?" asked Mags, "Why has he suddenly let her into his life?"

"What if I invite him around for lunch tomorrow and I'll see if I can find out what's going on?"

"Ohh, would you?" Mags almost squealed with delight. "I'd really appreciated it. It's just that, well with the private investigator work he does, I'm not really part of that, all I had was gardening time and I really like him."

"I understand." That she did, she'd been through all this with her children and their friends, as well as with Beth, who had a bad habit of pushing people away just as they were getting to know her.

There were three Christmas treats left on the plate, Mags took one and popped it in her mouth.

"Not bad," she said, "not as good as the treats Bob made last year." Nettie nodded, she had to agree with that, and what better way to get him around to her place the next day, than with an invitation to bake for her little Christmas Eve gathering in the shop. As Mags left by the back door, she sent a text, then went out into the shop to relieve Bron, all the time cooking up a plan to get Bob and Mags together by Christmas.

"Sometimes being a friend means mastering the art of timing. There is a time for silence. A time to let go and allow people to hurl themselves into their own destiny. And a time to prepare to pick up the pieces when it's all over."

- Octavia E. Butler

Bob Fletcher

Bob had gone inside to collect a cold drink for Nicki when his phone chimed. He checked the text, something was up, Molly had to see Nicki immediately.

He took the drink outside and was amused to see the young child standing with her hands on her hips surveying the finished borders. They'd spent the entire weekend planting and watering and now the front of the house and the fence border looked ready to present a glorious display over the next two to three weeks. He had been impressed with Nicki's stamina and concentration for one so young. She had green fingers and a love for nature that one.

Downing the last of her drink, Nicki had been so intent on what she had to do next, she didn't notice a car pull up in the street outside the front gate. As Molly entered the garden, Nicki turned and was surprised to see the visitor, her usual radiant smile turned immediately disappeared and she glared at Bob.

"It's not time to go yet," she said, her brows knitted together in a frown.

"I think Mrs Sykes has some news for you," said Bob quietly. He was hoping the news was good, it upset him to think that Nicki's time in Thornbury might be up.

Molly was a temporary caregiver and most of those in her care went back to parents or on to a permanent home within six months.

That meant it was near the end of Nicki's time in the Sykes household. A pain shot across Bob's chest as he thought of never seeing Nicki again.

"Hello," called Molly waving as she walked up the path towards the front door. Neither Bob nor Nicki said anything. "I've got some wonderful news," she called as she came closer to them.

Bob looked at Molly who was smiling, then at Nicki who was weary and hunched over. He took a step closer to Nicki, he wanted to protect the seven-year-old. Sometime over the past couple of weeks he had started to think of her as family.

"I've just heard from the hospital," said Molly looking directly at Nicki, "it's your Mum. She's woken up. It's still early but it's looking good. The doctors think that there isn't too much damage, and because she's young, they are expecting a full recovery. Isn't that wonderful?"

Nicki stood there looking at Molly Sykes, the scowl fixed firmly on her face saying nothing. Her hands were clenching and unclenching and Bob was confused.

"That's good news, isn't it?" he asked. Nicki turned and glared at him with such intensity he was surprised. Molly walked over to the child and took her hand.

"Let's sit and talk," she said calmly, "something is upsetting you. We can help."

Settling down on the verandah chairs Molly quietly explained to Nicki that nothing was going to change for now, but she can go and see her mother when the doctors say she can have visitors.

Bob had hoped that that would bring back the beautiful smile and the little Busy Bee would be back. But she wasn't and he didn't know what to do. Molly reached over and put her hand on his.

"It's ok, she's just processing this new information. It was a change that happened without, rather than within." Bob looked at Molly and nodded even though he had no idea what she was talking about. "I'll be going then. I'll let you know what our plans are, and we need to sort out what is happening next weekend with the gardening." With that she stood up and headed toward the car.

Nicki stood there staring at Molly, she still hadn't said a word. She looked over at Bob. He smiled.

"Do you want to go with Mrs Sykes?" he asked, "It's ok, you can stay or go, we've finished the important stuff for now, but there's some more …" Bob stopped mid-sentence.

The gardening gloves were pulled of the small hands and dropped on the ground and the straw hat pulled off and thrown down next to them. Nicki didn't turn to look at Bob again but followed Molly to the car, her head bowed and feet dragging. As the car pulled away, Bob saw her on her seat in the back. She didn't look his way, and as Nicki left with her foster parent Bob felt a piece of him had just gone missing.

A sudden breeze picked up in the garden, it had been a pleasant day but there was a sudden chill.

"Do you think she'll be alright?" he asked aloud to no-one. He wished Maud was here, she'd bring him back to earth with some common sense.

"I really care about her, I can't bear to think of her being unhappy, I'm sure now her mother is awake everything will be alright."

The breeze blew the heads of the roses that nodded in agreement with him. "But what if it's because of her mother, what was her life like before?" An uneasy feeling that something was missing crept over him and his mind started thinking of all the terrible things that could have happened to his young protégé.

He wandered around the garden going deeper into the 'what ifs' and catastrophising, so by the time he stopped walking he was in a state. He took a deep breath and try as he might he couldn't get back to the calm feeling he had earlier. A thought popped into his mind, Mags could help, she'd know what to do. She was a gardener too, so if Nicki couldn't …

No, he didn't even want to think of that, and Mags had seemed standoffish to Nicki when she called around. She didn't know anything about children, she wasn't' a mother so she couldn't help. His mind was spiralling downward and he felt a chill.

"What if I have to make a choice," he said to the plants as he walked back to the verandah. "Nicki or Mags, how will I decide?"

He picked up the gloves and hat that Nicki had been wearing. Would he put them back in the shed? But what if he didn't see her again? He wanted to talk to someone, and usually he would go to Mags, but was she the one to talk to about this? He wasn't sure.

An almighty crack resonated around the garden, and Bob looked up to see a branch fall from the trees at the back of his property. It crashed onto the grass, luckily missing the fence and the garden plants.

"That was weird," he said aloud. He looked down at the gloves and hat he was holding.

The thought came like a star shining through a hole in clouds in the night. He would continue leaving them with his gardening things in the porch, just in case she came back. In his mind he saw Nicki and her joie de vivre made him smile, filling him with warmth that pushed the feeling of doom out. The child had such a cheery and optimistic nature, he couldn't imagine this blow would knock her back for too long.

That was it, he decided to leave her gardening things in the porch. He had to believe that Molly could bring Nicki back from the dark place she was in now.

*"A garden is a grand teacher. It teaches patience
and careful watchfulness; it teaches industry and
thrift; above all it teaches entire trust."*

- Gertrude Jekyll

December- the second week

Sir Neville Emerson

"Mrs Sykes to see you Sir Neville," said Sarah walking into the office with Molly following behind.

"Hmm …" he replied, absently staring out the open French doors to the garden beyond. It was another cloudy but humid day. The gardener was riding the mower over the front lawn while Jennifer wheeled a barrow down the path between the flower beds. This was growing weather and keeping the weeds at bay in the formal garden was a full-time occupation.

"Sir Neville?" Mrs Sykes stood by his desk, waiting for him to turn around.

"Ahh, Molly," he exclaimed. "Great to see you, how are those livewires in your care? That Nicki is a bright one, isn't she? And how is Ford? Starting to settle in I hope."

It always amazed Molly that this man would remember the children's names from their meeting about the children's Christmas party.

"Ford and Hemi West have become friends, and they spend time together after school," started Molly.

"Good, good, young Hemi needs friends his own age. When he arrived in Thornbury, he only knew his Gran and then her friends who are all pensioners."

"You're right about Nicki, she's a bright one, and she's developing a love for gardening," continued Molly, as Sir Neville nodded. "She and Lou have been helping Bob create his Christmas Garden, it seems they are all learning a lot from each other."

"Excellent news. Come, walk with me in the fresh air," said Sir Neville standing and stretching out his arms. "Too much sitting down is no good for old bones." He stepped through the French doors and out onto the patio, Molly followed.

They strolled down the path to the lake near the back of the property as Molly spoke of Lou's ordeal and pending court case.

"I'd heard about it," said Sir Neville, slightly subdued, he found it difficult to understand how people could rationalise abusive behaviour towards young people. "Young Lou has a guardian angel looking out for her, otherwise Inspector Dowling wouldn't have been there."

"She's a young woman who hasn't got much in the way of possessions," said Molly, as she answered Sir Neville's questions about the kidnapping and what plans Lou had for the future. She explained the hard work that went into maintaining good marks at tech while working at 'Hush Sweet Charlotte' hairdressers, and that without a cellphone, it would make things difficult. As usual, Sir Neville listened intently, a slight tremor appeared in his left arm. Molly noticed it, but said nothing. The man worked too hard, she decided, and she hoped he'd take a break after the Christmas rush.

In silent contemplation they walked further along the lake where they came across Jennifer, the gardener's sister who often helped out at busy times. Her blonde hair tied up in a ponytail and she wore overalls, a tee shirt and thigh-high gumboots, as she stood in the pond raking out weed that was starting to block the flow into the lake.

At the far side of the lake was a park bench next to a weeping willow, where Molly and Sir Neville stopped for a rest. The sticky heat was draining.

"I wanted to tell you about Pam, Nicki's mother," started Molly. Sir Neville sat back and nodded; he closed his eyes as he listened to Molly explain about the devastation events that had led up Nicki coming into her care.

"Now Pam is awake I want Nicki to go and see her. It would do the world of good for both of them, but Nicki is refusing and I can't find out why." Molly took a deep sigh; it had been difficult the last couple of days and she'd almost given up. "I need some event or reason to have Pam and Nicki get together, neither knowing the other will be there, especially Nicki. I was thinking of the children's party this coming weekend but it could be too noisy and overwhelming for Pam. We need something else."

A couple of ducks flew in and landed on the lake, gliding over the still water together, they were followed by three more that looked unsteady with their landings and plopped into the water rather than the graceful slide of the first two. Sir Neville's eyes were narrowed against the bright reflection from the water.

"Then they must come to lunch on Christmas Day!" bellowed Sir Neville, a cheery grin on his face. His mind was on a roll, as he thought about reorganising that afternoon. He was in his element. "I enjoy Christmas Day lunch, seeing all the people in Thornbury who are on their own at this time of the year." Molly nodded. She could think of a couple of people who would be there, they looked forward to it every year.

"And anyone who usually has friends and family at Christmas but for some reason this year they don't," added Molly. "Bob was saying just the other day he would be on his own for Christmas, although I thought he'll spend it with Mags." Molly shrugged; they were an odd couple but they seemed to make each other happy. Sir Neville smiled but said nothing.

"I'm looking forward to the day already but we only have a couple of weeks to get this organised. We'll need to get onto this right now," he said. "What do I need to do?"

It was with a renewed spring in his step that Sir Neville stood up and strode off down the path back to the house, Molly struggled to keep up with him.

Entering his office, he turned to Sarah who sat at her desk working on the computer.

"We have a plan, a special surprise on Christmas Day," he started, as Sarah stopped what she was doing and listened to her boss.

He was back to his usual jovial self, which was a relief. There had been a few times when she became worried about him, something wasn't quite right and he seemed distracted. And then there were all those secret appointments, where had he been going, she wondered.

"At the Christmas Day lunch at the Hog and Frog I want to celebrate some special people. We have to organise a few extra guests, I'll give you the details, I'm sure you can handle it. How are the posters and advertising going? Molly, you'll let your network know as usual, won't you?"

Molly didn't get a chance to reply as Sir Neville was back at his desk busy looking through his phone directory.

"Already on it," said Sarah. "I'd mocked up some posters, I was just waiting for you to tell approve them."

It was Molly who stood in the middle of the room, surprised at Sarah's anticipation of the day, she was amazing and seemed to understand everything that needed to be done There was nothing left for her to do, it was probably time to leave. Sir Neville and Sarah continued planning the day and Molly was relieved to leave it in their hands. He smiled and nodded, Sarah was on his wavelength, it made his job so much easier, and he couldn't be prouder.

"Caterers, we just want cold lunch, buffet, nothing fancy just what anyone would have at home. Must have pavlova, it isn't Christmas without pavlova," said Sir Neville as he looked at Molly. His enthusiasm was infectious and soon they were all throwing in their ideas of what was needed for the day.

"Oh, and a tree, with a present for Pam," said Molly, "I doubt there is anyone to give her a present. Oh, and for Louise too. I get the feeling she's never had Christmas presents before, I guess that family of hers never celebrated Christmas, some groups don't. They probably just had to spend the day staying away from everyone," she said with distain.

"Oh, the poor thing," blurted out Sarah. She thought for a minute. "Lou, is she the young apprentice hairdresser at Charlotte's?" Molly nodded. "Likes the goth and emo look," Sarah added.

"Although she's looking a bit different at the moment, and I have to say it suits her," Molly was pleased Lou had decided to keep the brown hair colour for now.

"That's it then, Lou will be my project. You two can look after Nicki and her mother, said Sarah.

It was just after 1 pm when Molly left the Estate, turning down the invitation to lunch with Sir Neville, Rhonda the event planner who had arrived for the afternoon planning session, and Sarah. She needed to get back to her charges and start reminding everyone of the Christmas lunch.

Saying goodbye on the patio they all noticed a couple of piwakawaka, fantails, flitting from branch to branch in the large bushed next to the house.

"That's unusual," said Sarah, "they usually don't do that while people are here."

"A message, a loved one from beyond the grave is trying to tell you everything is going to be alright," said Rhonda, "I have it on good authority." With a smile she walked back into the house, while the other three watched the small birds and each thought of the loved ones in their life who had passed on. Unknown to two of them, they thought of the same person.

Nettie Sanderson

It was a subdued Bob Fletcher who sat at her kitchen table. Usually, he'd be fussing around her wanting to help in some way, especially when he was on his own, but today he seemed to have no interest in anything.

He'd accepted the invitation, the reply to her text arrived quite late in the day, when she'd almost forgotten about it. It was lucky that Mags and Sasha-Rose, were in the shop from 11 am to start on the new Christmas display, so she could slip home early to get lunch ready. There was a friendly rivalry going on with other shops for the best interior decorations, and Nettie was happy to leave it to the creative people.

With both Mags and Bob feeling ill at ease about their relationship, she knew it was up to her to make them snap out of it and she had a plan. With years of experience working in problem management, she had the tools she needed to sort this mess out.

First, get Bob on her good side, make him relaxed so he'd talk. It was easy to make one of his favourite salads, tuna pasta, with little cherry tomatoes and a few asparagus spears.

A pleasant stroll past the local bakery on her way home resulted in a fresh sour dough loaf, and a large slice of black forest cherry cake to share. She'd been overjoyed to see the typically 1980's desert, it had been decades since she'd had a piece.

It was wonderful that the vintage recipes coming back in style, and wondered if she had her old cook books still around. .

Throughout lunch, Nettie chatted about the Christmas Eve party that would be held in the shop for both knitting groups, customers, and staff. She asked for suggestions of treats they could provide and discussed what he could make for the day. Usually over enthusiastic about his baking and all the options he wanted to try, this time getting information from him was like pulling teeth. Hard work and painful.

It got to the stage that Nettie was losing patience with him. He didn't talk, just nodded, he didn't take notes, or even try to be interested. He sat there looking out to the garden, and saying nothing. As she put the coffee on the table next to the cake slices, she decided she'd had enough of his sulking.

"That's it Bob! What is the problem? You're like a wet week, all dark and dreary. You were bright and happy on Saturday when you came in with those new biscuits, what where they again?"

That had his attention, he looked up at the thin face of the woman he'd worked with several years ago, and immediately knew she meant business. He sat up straight and cleared his throat.

"It's, well, it's complicated," he started.

"Don't 'it's complicated' me, Robert Fletcher. You should know better than that. Breaking complicated up to manageable pieces is what we used to do!" Bob moved back in his chair, she may look delicate and have a quiet nature, but she could be fierce when roused.

It took a couple of glasses of wine, before Nettie got any sense out of Bob. He'd taken a shine to the child and enjoyed teaching her about gardening. Often Lou would join them and he had learnt a lot about colour matching from her.

While Bob explained how Nicki became withdrawn when Molly told her that she would be able to see her mother next weekend, Nettie topped up his glass. He was concerned about her, why didn't she want to see her mother now she was out of the coma. Bob absentmindedly took a sip. He had theories, and they ranged from sensible and nothing more than a sulky girl to a terrified child because of her past but unknown history.

'That's the way,' thought Nettie as she jotted each idea down on paper. All they had to do now was go through those ideas and weed the unlikely away from the probable. But with little information, it was going to be hard. 'I may have to call in Molly,' Nettie decided.

It was when Bob stopped talking and Nettie had a chance to sip her wine, that she realized he'd had three glasses to her half. She sat back and looked at him. His cheeks were flushed and he had a glazed look in his eyes.

"I wish I had grandchildren here in Fornbury," he said. Nettie smiled. "I mean Fornbury," he said again.

"I'll get us some nibbles; don't want you being arrested for drunk and disorderly at this time of the year."

As Nettie placed some crackers and pâté on the table as Bob gave a little sigh.

"Ooh, from the deli? The real deal?" he asked putting a generous spreading of pâté on a cracker and popping it in his mouth.

"What else Bob?" Nettie asked as she turned to look at him. His cheeks were redder than before and he looked down at his almost empty glass.

"I'd never spoken with Mags about children before, and, well, when she came around the other day and Nicki was there, she was very strange." Nettie said nothing and put some pate on a cracker.

"I got the feeling, she didn't like Nicki and that was … well, I don't know. I want Mags in my life, I'm very fond of her, but what if the girls have children? What if she hates children and they won't be welcome?" He stopped and gulped down the rest of his wine.

It was not the time to mention it but she thought Bob's daughter, Agnetha Rhodes would never have children. They are too messy for her and her pompous husband, and youngest daughter, Diane, was living a good full life in Sydney and was still a long way from settling down.

"I think Mags puts on a tough face when she's unsure of the situation. Did she know about Nicki and Molly coming to your house in the weekends?" Nettie asked. Bob shook his head.

"It hadn't crossed my mind to tell her, but we talked about it after the knitting groups. She never said anything, but she was quieter than usual." Nettie raised an eyebrow.

"Do you think it's just cause she's mad at you?" asked Nettie deciding that attack is the best form of defense in this case. "You didn't tell her or even invite her to join in. You know she's a gardener, she may just be put out?"

"Oh, I hadn't thought of that," said Bob. He looked down at his empty glass. Nettie noticed but she ignored it.

"I asked her to help with the Christmas Garden last year, and now…"

"I'll bet she feels you've replaced her. And have you two been out together in the last few weeks?" Nettie knew the answer but she needed Bob to realise there were two people in his relationship with Mags.

"Oh, no," he replied a look of distress on his face. "Mags came and asked me to a Christmas do, and I said no because I was busy and then when she wanted to go for a walk, I said I couldn't cause I was working in the garden."

"I think you're starting to see the problem, and it's not Nicki." Nettie raised her eyes and looked at Bob over the top of her glasses. He nodded.

"I'm going to have to make this right," he said. "I guess I need to go and talk to her."

"And maybe a nice cooked dinner as well. You know she may have some insight into what is troubling Nicki, Mags has a wealth of experience from all sorts of places."

A loud thunk on the deck made them both look up, followed by scratching and huffing noises. A furry black head appeared by the step followed by an ear-piercing meow.

Nettie and Bob were transfixed, as the petite Prissy slowly walked up the steps at the side heaving something in her mouth that was almost the same size as her. It looked like a raw half chicken and Nettie was horrified.

"Where did you get that!" she demanded of the petite cat. "Oh dear, looks like someone has lost their dinner for this evening." Bob sat back and roared with laughter.

"Well, looks like we both have a chore this afternoon. You need to talk to Mags, and I need to find out where that chicken came from."

Beth Brookhurst

"Looking forward to retirement?" Ed, the project manager asked, grinning as he sipped a short black in his eco-friendly reusable cup. "No more meetings, belligerent support staff and vendor tantrums. I envy you."

"Oh yes, definitely," replied Beth, forcing a smile, "I can't wait."

Liar, she thought to herself as she walked to her desk and settled into the chair and switched on her computer, as part of her morning ritual. If only he knew.

She swivelled her chair to face the window which overlooked Wellington harbour. From level eight the view was beautiful, she could feel herself becoming emotional. The glistening water in the sunlight, dolphins and whales would sometimes appear in the harbour, sailboats and sea kayaks, joggers and food trucks along the waterfront and Kitts Park playground for the children. At this time of the year festive decorations were going up, the days were warmer and the summertime vibe had arrived. The thought that it was almost the last time she would be here made her feel slightly nauseated.

"Beth!"

Turning away from the window she could see a hand waving from across the room. It was Richard O'Shea, her replacement.

She had been training him in her role for the last fortnight, he came with all the right qualifications and overseas experience. It was his booming Irish voice that made him memorable. He had a mixture of wacky techniques and charm that the vendors loved, and he'd pulled the floundering account out of the doldrums.

She waved back and quickly scanned her appointments hoping she wasn't late for one. She didn't know what it was, but Richard ruffled her. He'd gotten under her skin and made her feel and think about things differently when she was around him. Since he had arrived, she'd found herself questioning her ideas and beliefs. On occasions she even questioned her own decisions.

She forced the thought to the back of her mind where it belonged. Flirtation and romance were best left between the pages of books and in movies. She leaned forward to study her emails.

A group had gathered around Richard, young, fresh, eager to do well in the world, full of enthusiasm and hope. If only she could feel like that now. Her hope had deserted her, and her world outside the office had shrunk since her neighbour and best friend, Nettie had left to start a business and a new life in Thornbury two years ago.

The thought of having to take retirement now and leave this organisation, was scary. More than that, thought Beth as she accepted another meeting for the project she was working on, it was downright terrifying.

She started working on the spreadsheet for the 10.30 meeting, and suddenly she felt calm. She was working, this she could cope with while the real world was still three days away.

At lunchtime her boss had organised a team get together at The Green Man. Usually Beth would shy away from these social events, but she liked that particular pub, they had great food. As she had no meetings this afternoon with Richard already taking responsibility for most of the work, she was going to treat herself with a glass of Rosé wine. She had barely settled in her seat before it began.

"Looking forward to retirement then?" asked one of the project administrators.

"I can't wait" Beth replied, the smile on her face didn't match her feelings. "I'll be thinking of you next week, slogging away while I sip coffee on my deck while reading a book."

One of the account managers looked enviously at her.

'That was me a decade ago,' Beth thought, 'imagining what I'd do when the magic retirement age came. All those adventures, all those plans…'

Now Beth was at that age, it was a different matter. Back then, she had her Aunt Ruth and her neighbour Nettie. Someone to share it all with. But her aunt's death from a stroke the same year that Nettie up and moved to Thornbury, hadn't just been a shock, it had been an earthquake. Her lively aunt was a substitute parent, they'd grown close, gossiped, cried, laughed, and become great friends. Losing touch for a while, Beth had come to her rescue when she became sick and took her small dogs in, there was no one else to care. The sad part was that once she entered the rest home, her health and her enthusiasm for life rapidly went downhill.

Then there was Nettie. They'd been neighbours and then best friends for years. Beth was a surrogate aunt for Nettie and Alex's children, which she, secretly, enjoyed and felt honoured to be part of the family. After Nettie and Alex split up and Alex moving out after the children had left home, Nettie and Beth's friendship grew stronger. They'd created plans, places to travel to things they wanted to do, their bucket lists. The thought of attempting even half of them without her best friend or aunt was overwhelming.

"There's more changes ahead," Christine their section manager was saying, "I can't believe it, how many restructures can one organisation take in a year?"

While Beth knew Christine thought she was being kind moving the topic away from her, hearing the others complain about the changes only made the feeling that all this, her safety net, was being pulled from under her feet. She was no longer going to be part of this team, she realised as they whinged away. The impending fear of the inevitable washed over her, she wasn't ready for the end of her work life.

It was only Richard that talked up the changes putting a positive spin on it all. Hearing him enthuse over the way it would all make their customer engagement better was inspiring. He couldn't be that much younger than her, but he accepted change more readily than some of the younger members of the organisation.

She watched him gesticulate on the new workflow and software they would be using with such passion, she found herself getting caught up in the moment. At some point she brought herself back to reality but was startled to see him staring at her.

Their eyes locked, and Beth immediately felt unsettled. She'd been smiling. She turned away hoping no one would notice the flush in her cheeks. How long had it been since she was near someone so passionate, it had been a very long time she realised.

"You're better out of it," said Resis, one of her colleagues who would have been in their late twenties.

"Too right," she replied on autopilot.

Resis looked at Beth, "I know you're looking forward to finishing, but we'll miss you. You're fabulous at your job, and the customers all love you." Beth raised an eyebrow. "Oh, yes we're expendable, you know what the customers are like, short memories and a restructure and it'll be someone new, who jumps at their commands." Beth was surprised to hear Resis's voice thick with emotion.

"Oh, all venders are expendable, added Beth, "they'll find the next new funky software and workflow to sell, and then they'll be irreplaceable." She said that a bit too loudly as she looked over at Richard. It was a low blow, but she couldn't help it. It doesn't matter how you dress it up it was just wrong. What was the point in putting another new system in place when the old one had the same functions, but wasn't used properly? All she could see was a new broom sweeping clean, that which could be recycled.

On their way back to the office, Beth felt a hand on her shoulder. It was Richard.

"I heard what you said back there," he said smiling.

Beth nodded and could feel heat rising in her cheeks as her instant response was to get ready to defend herself. She was sure he would challenge her over what she said.

"You'll never be expendable," Richard said, "your knowledge and skills will always …"

She didn't hear the rest of his sentence, her legs were moving on autopilot, sweeping her away and into the stairwell. 'What is wrong with me?' she wondered. She pushed open the door into the woman's rest rooms, and as she stood staring at herself in the mirror, she realised exactly what it was. She felt her life was out of control, that someone else was directing it and she was starting to run down, like a redundant part.

Her last two days had been full of writing documentation, making sure processes and info sheets were up to date. It had taken time to make sure the documents were succinct and as precise as possible, although she could think of at least one person in her team who would complain that they were hard to follow and try and rewrite them. This would no longer be her problem. A weight lifted from her shoulders as she handed the updated documentation to the knowledge manager, who thanked her and promptly added it to his 'to do' list. Beth was quite convinced it would never be looked at again, even when there was a crisis. She knew how the organisation worked.

On Friday at 4pm on the dot, she logged out of the network for the last time and was ready to leave when their division manager entered the floor.

Clinking and rustling noises were heard in the kitchen, such was the wonder of open plan, and Beth groaned inwardly. All she wanted to do was sneak out the back way and go home.

Instead, there were speeches, gifts, drinks, and nibbles. Her face was tired, constantly stretched in a smile, she had to rub her lips together every now and then to ease the pain. When the division manager left, many colleagues did the same, but she felt she had to stay with her team, who looked like they had settled in for a while.

It was almost 6pm when the last of them decided to go and get something to eat before they went on to a karaoke bar. Now was the time for Beth to escape and in the surge of people on the street, she slipped away toward the train station.

Evening trains on Friday's had the exhausted and the drunk. It was a slow journey, having missed the last express train to the Hutt, but while ignoring people she started thinking about what she would do come Monday. Her stomach felt like there was a deep black hole that was sucking all the life from her. She'd never let herself be taken over by destructive negative feelings before. She was a 'up and at 'em' kind of person, she needed to pull her socks up, put on her big girl panties and change her attitude. No good ever came from wallowing.

On arriving home, she grabbed the mail from the letterbox and opened the front door, and was greeted by one slightly confused black and white papillon and one limping Pomeranian.

Both little dogs were now of an age where they had reached double figures, and health problems were creeping in. Arthritis was talking its toll on Twinkle, while poor old Pepi le Peuh seemed to be daily surprised at some familiar object or event and had lost most of his teeth.

After cuddles and hugs, the dogs were fed and everyone was settled in front of the television. There was nothing Beth wanted to watch, so she went to the doggy channel and her large screen came alive with a jaunty tune and images of young fit dogs bouncing around fields, playing chase and fetch the stick. This channel seemed to be a favourite, and the two dogs now sat on the couch transfixed by the images racing around the screen.

With a sigh, Beth picked up the mail, some circulars which went in the bin, a letter from the bank about a term deposit, and a couple of envelopes that looked like cards. She opened one with a feeling of dread.

As she stared at the image of a Christmas tree decked out in colourful lights and baubles, she realised how close it was to Christmas. Somehow it had completely slipped her mind. A realisation that she would have been off work in two weeks' time for the Christmas break hit her. There it was! The foothold she'd been searching for, she could start making plans, and from there she could find new interests and another occupation to fill in the void of now longer being at work.

It was a warm feeling that surrounded her as she read the card, her cousin Lizzie had invited her over to stay for a couple of days at Christmas. She would accept, after all, Thornbury wasn't too far away and she could catch up with Nettie.

On opening the second envelope, Beth couldn't believe it, but she held a card from Nettie showing a wreath of candles and holly, which also had an invitation over Christmas.

"I'm popular today," said Beth to Twinkle and Pepi, both ignored her, but for the first time in weeks, Beth felt excited about the future.

December- the third week

"Christmas is most truly Christmas when we celebrate it by giving the light of love to those who need it most."

- Ruth Carter Stapleton

Ford, Nicki, Molly Sykes and Louise

"Now remember," said Mrs Sykes pulling up outside the Thornbury school gate, "Mrs West, Hemi's Nan is picking you up today. You're to go to her place until I get back from court."

The two children sitting on their booster seats in the back of the car nodded. "Ford, can you remember to be a good boy and remember to say please and thank you?"

The child shifted in his seat and shrugged.

"If the court case goes on until tomorrow, we will have to stay in Wellington for the night, and you will have a sleep over at Mrs Wests house. Remember we talked about this last night. Do you remember what to do?" Nicki nodded enthusiastically and Ford looked out the window. Molly Sykes got out of the car and helped both of them out of their booster seats, handed them their school bags containing packed lunches and said goodbye. Nicki always liked a hug, and the seven-year-old skipped away happy to be at school and knowing where everyone was. Molly was pleased, the Christmas party in the weekend had brought joy and happiness back to the child, and it seemed she was now back to her old self.

It was a different story for Ford, he enjoyed the party, but he was still wary of everyone and everything. He knew, without a doubt, that if Mrs Sykes went away, he wouldn't see her again.

From everything that was happening, he concluded that he and Nicki were going to live with Mrs West now, because that's what usually happened at all the other foster homes, he'd been in. But this time it wouldn't be so bad, he liked Hemi, they had become friends in his time at Thornbury, and Mrs West was ok. It could be worse. It was time he was moved on anyway; he'd been at Mrs Sykes house for almost four weeks, way longer than anywhere else.

Standing looking at the school he wondered why he had to go there, he didn't like it much. Some of the kids made fun of him because he couldn't read and write and he was no good at maths. Others called him names because he was a foster kid.

"It's the last week of school before holidays," said Mrs Sykes, "only three more days to go. There will be fun stuff to do this week, I think you'll enjoy it. I'll phone this evening if I'm away and you can tell me all about it. How would you like that?"

Ford shrugged again and Molly Sykes desperately wanted to hug the underweight, short eight-year-old. She put her hand gently on his shoulder and felt him tremble at her touch. At least he didn't run away from it now. It would just take time. The school bell rang.

"Off you go and have a great day," she said.

Without looking back, Ford walked toward the main school building where students were starting to form lines outside the class rooms. "Keep safe and may the angels shine their light with love and healing for you" said Molly, softly so no one around her heard.

After Ford had walked through the door, Molly got into the car and looked at the passenger at her side. "Are you ready for this?" she asked.

"Yes," was the firm reply, "if I can stop what happened to me from happening to my sisters and any others then it will be worth it."

"Then on to Wellington and court it is. I'm there for you and Inspector Dowling and Officer Jamie will be there as witnesses, you won't be alone. Remember you are very brave, and smart. It was your quick thinking that kept you from being shipped off to who knows where."

Nodding, Louise swallowed hard. She'd have to relive that nightmare. It had been because of the 'keep yourself safe' modules she did in both courses, she didn't think much of them at the time. It had surprised her that she'd remembered enough information to escape when those men tried to take her.

A slight flush rose in her cheeks when she recalled her complaints about the module, telling her tutor she'd never need the information and didn't see any point in it. A smile did cross her face as she thought of how attentive they were in one class, the lessons on escaping from a hostage situation, mainly because of the handsome police officer who conducted it. Never in her wildest dreams occurred to her that she'd have to use the information.

The two men who accosted her had no idea she'd be ready for them, because of what she'd learnt, preparing the students for work in big international and sometimes controversial industries.

Over the past week, she'd been helped by Mrs Sykes, it was going to be difficult to testify against the religious group her family belonged. But she was becoming more confident.

They picked the wrong person when they approached her.

Lou still felt embarrassed that she went with them in the first place. Knowing they were members of the religious group should have rung warning bells for her. Thinking back, she had felt uneasy but she so badly wanted to see her siblings, it never occurred to her she was in danger.

The religious group had a dark secret, and Lou wondered if her parents knew. If they did, she would never forgive them. The two men thought she was on her own, alone, lost and easily manipulated. But thanks to Bob Fletcher and Molly Sykes, she was now a ward of the state and under care.

She wasn't just another troubled runaway teen from a toxic home, thinking that once they had broken her spirit, they could smuggle her out of the country. A shudder went down her spine as she realised how close she'd been to arriving alone in an unknown overseas destination as part their human trafficking trade.

But they'd been wrong. Molly Sykes, and Charlotte her boss, Bob and the Stick Chick knitters at Nettie's Knit Shop, they all cared about her, and that kept her going.

It was unbelievable to Lou that Inspector Dowling had the operation under surveillance and that he recognised her. And when she got away, he'd followed the kidnapper's car to the railway station. She hadn't seen him there, but if she had, she wasn't sure if she'd have the courage to talk to him.

She decided he was her guardian angel that day, especially after she found out he had left a police officer at the station to make sure they didn't drag her out.

Meanwhile he took his car and sped over the Remutuka hill, alerting Officer Jamie, both arriving at the Thornbury station just in time.

Relaxing back in her seat, Lou gave Molly a smile. "Thank you," she said just as Molly's phone chimed indicating a text. Molly asked Lou to check the message for her and smiled.

"That's cool," she said, "Charlotte has just sent a text wishing me luck. She's great, isn't she?" Molly nodded and agreed. Charlotte had been an inspirational boss, making sure Louise had all the technical skills for her hairdressing exams and letting her have time off for visits to the police, lawyers, and now for the court case. If it was inconvenient at this time of the year, Charlotte didn't mention it once.

Driving on through Featherston, the decorations in the street and lights were quite magical.

"I'm sorry you missed the party on Saturday, having to work. Sir Neville always puts on a wonderful Christmas party for the foster kids, careers and other kids in need. He's so generous, the party, the toys, he pays for it all himself. It would be a bleak time for some if it wasn't for him.

"That's ok," replied Lou, "we never celebrated Christmas the way everyone else did. I'd never seen a tree in a house before until we all put yours up on Friday."

"It's not a time for presents, actually in our faith, you don't get to celebrate anything. There is always something sad or horrifying around each of the events everyone else celebrates. We were told only heathens and pagans celebrate. We had to pray."

She shivered at the thought and kept looking ahead out the window watching the road ahead.

There wasn't a lot to say about that, and Molly spend the rest of the trip thinking about what they were going to do to bring some joy into this teen's life. It sounded as if it had been tough from day one, and her recent ordeal was traumatic. Molly knew that there would be a party that Lou would never forget, but first things first. Getting through the preliminaries of this court case and then they could relax and celebrate.

'If you can't enjoy life and help people at the same time, then what is the point,' she though as they headed for Wellington.

Mark and Mandy Weatherby

When Sir Neville came to them with the party information, Mark was cautious, worried that Mandy would be overwhelmed.

"I don't think Mandy is up to hosting an event like that, and not on Christmas Day. It's one of the two days we get to close, and the radiation therapy is starting to take a toll on her." Fatigue and some skin damage around the targeted area had started showing up, causing concern to both of them, but was brushed off by the nurses as being normal. It didn't help being told other people had worse symptoms, Mark was getting annoyed with the unsympathetic staff they had dealings with, and was starting to tell them so.

"It will all be arranged by Sarah, Rhonda and myself with a team of elves. No cooking needed, it's all cold and buffet style. I've put in an order for a lovely hot day." Sir Neville chuckled. "If you have someone who wants to work a few hours at the bar, for double time pay, I'm happy to take them on. Don't worry about clean up. That will be all sorted by my team. All you two have to do is sit back and enjoy the day, oh and be my Santa's helpers, what do you say?"

Mark looked to Mandy who was just gaping at Sir Neville, her mouth open, eyes wide.

"You have people already organised for this?" she asked, trying to cope with the magnitude of getting everything organised the way she normally would, just one week out from Christmas.

"The joys of having staff," Sir Neville replied, "they'll have everything prepared. We have eco-friendly disposable napkins, crockery and cutlery, so it can all be put in the one bag at clean-up for recycling in the composter at Washburn estate. We're trialling a new product; this will be its biggest test."

"I don't know, the noise, all the people, I get so tired ..." said Mandy looking to Mark for support.

"All oldies, or people on their own. We will have Nicki for a little while, but the plan is for her to come in with Molly during the afternoon when the presents are being given out."

Mark and Mandy both looked at Sir Neville and then at Sarah who was sitting quietly as usual taking notes.

After a furtive glance around the room, Sir Neville moved his chair closer into the table where they were sitting in the bar of the Hog and Frog. "There's a plan," he whispered.

Over the next half hour, he and Sarah explained the series of events that had been arranged for two specific purposes. One, to get Nicki and her mother together and the other to give Lou her very first Christmas celebration. It was the turning point in the conversation. When Mandy heard the plight of Lou and Nicki, she gave in.

"We have to help Sir Neville do this," Mandy told Mark. "How awful for Pam, not knowing if she'll see Nicki again and worse, not knowing why. And as for Lou, we can give her a great day, can't we?" Mark nodded, all he wanted to do was make Mandy happy and to keep her safe. If this was going to bring some joy in her life, then he was all for it.

"I know Bron and Rick are going to his parents for Christmas so they won't be around, I'll ask Heather, and Ross is back from Uni, looking for extra work. I'm sure he'd jump at some double time work. I'll send them texts," said Mark. He also was amazed at how Sir Neville could pull together all those staff on Christmas Day.

"What about advertising?" asked Mandy, "has it started?"

"We have posters around the town, where the lonely and alone go, notice boards, shops, and if you can put one up here in the bar, we'd be grateful," said Sarah handing over two glossy A3 posters. "It's just for locals, so it will be a small affair" she continued.

"If you know of any who may fit the bill, let them know," said Sir Neville indicating the retired group in the corner playing cards.

"Is that it?" asked Sir Neville, "have we left anything out?" He looked to Sarah who scanned over her notes.

"All covered. I'll have the decorators in over the next couple of days to decorate the restaurant areas. I hope you don't mind, but Sir Neville insisted in a massive tree to impress Lou," said Sarah chuckling, and the way she looked at Sir Neville, struck Mandy. She looked at him like a beloved father, even their features were similar. If she hadn't been so tired, she would have thought more about it, but today was a bad day and after this meeting she need a lie down.

"We're delighted. Decorating has been low on our priority list this year as you can see," Mark waved his arm around to the sparse decorations that gave the hint it might be Christmas. Sarah jotted down some notes and smiled.

As Sir Neville and Sarah left, Mark helped Mandy to the staff staircase at the back of the building.

"I just had a thought," said Mark, "has John replied? Do we know what he's doing for Christmas?"

With a weary smile, Mandy shook her head. "I haven't heard if he is or not, it all depends on this case he's working on. He's in for a bit of a surprise if he arrives on Christmas day." A large smile crossed Mandy's face and Mark was pleased that she had something to look forward to in the near future.

"I need to pop in to see Charlotte," said Sarah as they left the Hog and Frog.

"I'll come with you, I want to see the accessibility accesses we put in, starting with the one here. Then I should visit Nettie." Sir Neville pursed his lips, "I said I would visit her shop when we chatted at the post-Christmas party at Washburn last year, but I'm sad to say, I never made it."

The new wheelchair and accessibility entrance was at the side of the Hog and Frog, after the council refused to let the contractors build it from the footpath. That decision had caused Sir Neville and the architect to come up with something even better. The old original door into the bar remained, but now a new modern, but keeping with the style of the building door was becoming more popular. The entrance was 'charmingly rustic', as reported by their local rugby hero and news hound, Trevor Clarke, but the biggest asset was it was sheltered from the elements while having easy access doors for those in wheelchairs, with crutches, walking sticks or in the need of a service dog.

It entered into what had been a dingy back room used by servants back in the day, and until recently, used as a storage room. It was now repurposed as an open area where coats could be removed in peace and then a direct path into the dining room, past the bar on one side and the kitchen on the other.

A feeling of pride came over Sir Neville as he looked at the new ramp, he always knew owning a few of the historic buildings in the small town would end up being expensive, but it was about giving back to the community and it gave him a sense of belonging. The area had been previously neglected as the back side of the building. Now it was filled with native plants and a few outdoor seats, that complimented the view of the Thornbury Pond in the centre of The Crescent. He knew there would eventually be some more tweaks needed, but for now, the local Disability organisation had given their approval, and he was satisfied with that.

Walking around The Crescent, past the entrance to the shopping mall, the Council chambers and town hall, they walked up the rise to the walkway in front of The Mews shopping precent, another of his buildings.

"They've done a good job with the decoration, earthquake strengthening and accessibility here too," said Sir Neville. It had cost him a fortune, but it was necessary and his tenants safety was more important than money. They waved hello and a Merry Christmas to Lois and Jillian in the real estate office. Then called in for a quick chat with Nancy Scott owner operator of 'Velvet Silk Boutique' quality garments for the discerning woman, specialising in mother-of-the-bride and mother-of-the-groom dresses.

Sir Neville was pleased to see, Nancy was branching out with a few men's wear items, locally made, and told Sarah to make a note of it when looking for a new tie. Resisting the urge to settle at a table for coffee and a cake at the Lemon Strawberry Café, he went in just to check with the chef and Lizzie instead. Both were delighted to see him, as he reminded them of his yearly party between Christmas and New Years for the businesses of Thornbury.

Sarah slipped into 'Hush Sweet Charlotte' hairdressers as Sir Neville waved to Charlotte through the window, and then moved on to Nettie's knit shop.

The small bell over the front door tinkled as the door creaked open, and the imposing figure of Sir Neville entered. Mags gave an audible gasp to see him in the shop. Nettie had been in the kitchen and stopped in her tracks when she saw him.

"This is very festive," he said looking around at the knitted and crocheted items on display next to tinsel and other Christmassy decorations. "There's a theme, cause I'm assuming you have entered in the competition," he said smiling. Mags nodded enthusiastically. "Wait, don't tell me, let me guess." He walked around the shop, stopping at each group of decorations as he did. About halfway around he smiled and then laughed, but continued on his journey around the shop to the separate decorative groups.

"It's the 12 Days of Christmas," he said with a large smile on his face.

"Yes. That's it," replied Mags, it was Sasha-Rose's idea."

"Sasha-Rose? Would that be Amber-May's daughter? She seems a little young to be helping out in the shop."

"She's seventeen and off to tech next year," said Nettie walking into the shop, "they grow up so quickly."

"Yes, that they do," replied Sir Neville, "I was thinking she must be about ten or eleven now. That's how out of touch I am," he chuckled. "Well now, I managed to visit, just as I said I would," he said with a sly smile, "better late than never, eh?" He walked to the window where the knitting groups would gather and sat down on the couch. "I hear your knitting groups are great fun and you have some characters coming along to them." Nettie's eyes grew wide, how did he know that, she wondered.

"Yes," she replied, "some great knitters and quite a few beginners. Great characters, one or two of them definitely," she said with a smile.

Not long after Sarah entered the shop, and Sir Neville challenged her to find the shop theme. It took her even less time to work out what it was. "It's very clear, and so beautiful. I particular like the seven swans a swimming," she added,

Nettie showed her the new decorations from Sasha-Rose and Sarah almost squealed with delight. She purchased several, and told them all they would be the decorative highlight in her lounge. Sir Neville smiled and wondered if Sarah had purchased more than she needed, and if there were a couple of decoration to be added to a special Christmas present.

Magnolia (Mags) Wild

"This place is stark and dreary; you certainly aren't trying to impress anyone."

Barbara Wild entered the dim hallway and set her bag on the wooden floor, next to the single bedroom that would be hers for the next couple of days. Mags bit her lip and closed the door behind her aunt, hoping she could keep calm for the short time they would share this one bedroomed cottage near the edge of the town.

Following Mags to the rear of the building, Aunt Barbara managed to inspect nooks and crannies for dust as she walked through the hallway. A blue plastic holder with air freshener hung discreetly from the picture rail behind the door to what once would have been the parlour. The seventy-year-old woman stopped and glared at the offending item. Pulling her shoulders back at attention, she whipped the plastic container from the wall and held it at arm's length as though it were a pair of smelly socks.

"It's dark here, doesn't get any sunlight and I wanted to make it fresh," explained Mags, desperately trying to avoid the fact she was trying to cover up a musty, mouldy smell.

"Nonsense," Aunt Barbara said as she dropped the air freshener in the rubbish basket.

"You should know better. If people see plastic knick-knacks, they might get the wrong idea. You're a good gardener by all accounts, there should be a vase of fresh flowers on a hall table."

Then she gave Mags a smile that from anyone else would have been considered patronising, and Mags would have told them just what they could do with their fresh flowers. But this was Aunt Barbara, and Mags knew it was just her way.

"Happy Christmas, Magnolia." She enfolded Mags into her arms. "It's lovely to see you." Aunt Barbara was her great aunt, the only child from her grandfather's second marriage, stuck in the middle, older than her nieces and nephews, but much younger than her half-siblings.

A career woman from the time she left school at 16, joining the forces. She had done well serving in the Navy, but since she retired over 15 years ago, it had been a tradition that she would arrive on December 20 and leave after brunch on Christmas Eve. Mags, her sibling, Rowan, and the cousins on Aunt Barbara's side, found the habit amusing and as she visited but once every five years, they let it continue. They would never admit it but they were all quite fond of the old duck.

Mags's brother, Rowan was much older than her, and looked forward to Aunt Barbara's visits. He let her boss him about and she could get away with anything. But Mags was too much like the feisty woman herself, and struggled with being told what to do.

At the last visit, they tried to compromise, but it didn't work, Mags had to bite her tongue and put up with it. It was especially hard as her aunt keep pointing out she just didn't have the 'laid back' gene. As if it wasn't already obvious Mags was nothing like her brother. Rowan and Aunt Barbara would spend hours poring over photo albums, reminiscing about people and places that Mags cared nothing about. When Aunt Barbara visited Rowan, they spent their time wrapped up in their-own little world.

"Where's your tree?" she asked walking from the parlour to the kitchen/dining area, out to the enclosed sundeck and back into the parlour.

"I don't bother. It's not worth it when there's only me," replied Mags.

"You must have a tree," she said in a voice that allowed no argument. "We'll get one this afternoon."

"There's no need. I found an artificial one just in case …"

Barbara Wild folded her arms.

"Well, don't just stand there. Go and fetch it. And don't forget to bring the decorations."

Mags had an urge to click her heels and salute, her aunt spoke with such authority. After years managing and ordering divisions and sailors, Mags knew was just her way, but it went against everything she had fought for in her life.

Out in the sunroom, under the spare bed, Mags had put the boxes of Christmas stuff, hoping she wouldn't need them. It had been Bob who suggested they went to a second-hand shop in Masterton and see if there was anything suitable.

It had been a difficult couple of weeks with Bob but talking out their feelings had certainly helped. Mags felt even closer to him, and decided she had to trust him, as things would progress in their own time.

It wasn't something Mags did, decorate for Christmas, but Bob had years of experience and knew what was needed. He got her to think back on the last Aunt Barbara visit, until he got an idea of what would go well to satisfy the elderly woman.

With care, Mags pulled the boxes out from under the bed and carried them carefully to the table in the kitchen. Unnoticed before, Mags saw they were all labelled in neat and precise handwriting, they had once been cherished.

As Mags open opened the lids, she wondered about the family that used this tree and its associated baubles, she picked up one of the glass ornaments and saw written in glitter 'Baby's first Xmas', a lump came to her throat and she quickly put the bauble back in the box.

How long had it been, she wondered, well over 20 years, and every day of every one of them she had remembered, and wondered. But that was gone, time had passed and nothing could change it back. She just had to get on with life, make it as full of happiness, laughter and good times as she could. They had gone, and that was that.

As soon as Aunt Barbara saw the well-loved, imitation pine tree, she insisted they put it up, and then decorate it. That translated into Aunt Barbara put it up while Mags handed branches and various implements to make it sturdy.

Once the last of it was assembled, Mags put the box that held the tree back under the spare bed, while Aunt Barbara found a suitable place for it to stand and then started with the decoration. All Mags could do in the end was watch, offer approving comments and make a pot of tea with a plate of Bob's Christmas shortbread biscuits that he had made especially for the visit.

While Mags was making another pot of tea and wondering if she should start getting organising something for lunch, she could hear Aunt Barbara singing 'Deck the halls', Mags smiled. She was certainly in good spirits and she walked back into the room to find her aunt hanging a string of lights in the window that looked out toward the road.

Mags was horrified. She hadn't realised there were lights in the box. Her mind spun as she thought of excuses, how could she stop her aunt from putting the lights up.

"I won't be able to pull the curtains properly," Mags pointed out. "I think they should go in the kitchen instead; it could do with a bit of festive decoration."

For the next two days, Aunt Barbara took charge. The meagre tree ornaments were increased by iced gingerbread stars with silver balls. Paper chains were made and strung around the rooms, the parlour, kitchen and hallway. When her aunt had first suggested it, Mags had smiled and secretly rolled her eyes, but funnily enough, she found she had enjoyed every minute.

The front door entrance had never looked so good, Aunt Barbara insisted the door stayed open to allow sunlight into the gloomy hallway.

It was as if the cottage had been deprived for decades and had now found a new lease on life.

A small side table from Mags' room was put in the hall and Aunt Barbara created a festive floral display with pine fronds and flowers from the garden. The pine scent and colourful blooms raised their spirits and Mags, who never cared about celebrating Christmas, felt wrapped up in the season.

On the days Mags was in Nettie's Knit Shop, Aunt Barbara walked into the town centre with her. Always one to take a brisk constitutional after dinner, the seventy-year-old was no stranger to long walks. The weather had been delightful and Aunt Barbara enjoyed browsing around the shops, having a treat at the Yellow Strawberry Café, rummaging through the books at A Readers Dream in the mall, then sitting down by the duckpond in the middle of The Crescent to read her latest purchase. Sometimes she would delve through the dark recess that held boxes of bric-a-brack at Tim's Emporium. When she felt like company she would come into the shop for a bit of a chat or pop into the Hog and Frog for a natter with the locals and a cooling lemonade.

Even though Mags had been dreading her turn with Aunt Barbara, she'd found the whole four days, pleasantly refreshing and she felt alive and renewed, able to cope with the usually stressful end of year chaos. For the first time in years, Mags felt the whole tedious Christmas season might not be so bad after all.

On her last night, Aunt Barbara produced a bottle of Irish Cream after dinner and she sat Mags down next to her on the two-seater couch in front of the Christmas tree for a heart to heart.

"This time of year, must be hard for you, being so far away from your family," she said with a smile that made Mags feel like a child that couldn't be trusted on their own. "I'm sure you have wonderful friends, but family is special, isn't it?" She put her hand on Mags and took a deep breath. "I'm staying with family on my mother's side over Christmas, I could ask if they have room for one more. They've got a big house."

"Thanks Aunt Barbara, but I'll be fine," said Mags, then just to bring the point home added, "I have plans." She nodded.

"I've been working as a volunteer at archives you know," she started, "it keeps me busy and my mind sharp." Mags smiled, she wondered if Aunt Barbara's mind would ever dull. "And in my time there, I've found some, well shall we say, useful contacts."

Mags took a sip of the Irish Cream and felt the warmth go down her throat. She wondered where her aunt was going with her story.

"I don't know if you know that I know," said Aunt Barbara, gulping the Irish cream down in one gulp and pouring herself another. "I guess I should have mentioned it before, but I just thought it wasn't appropriate. I had nothing to say to you on the matter." Mags could feel her heart pounding and suddenly her throat felt dry. She gulped down her drink and held it out for another.

"How old would you have been, 17 or 18?"

Mags froze, she was 16 years old and the memories were starting to flood back, no matter how hard she tried to suppress them. She hadn't spoken to anyone of this, and she wondered how Aunt Barbara knew.

Then it dawned on her, the family gathering, the call to action that had happened at the time. It would have been her mother, making the rest of the family see how much Mags had shamed the family. Even though they were in the mid 1990's when being a single unmarried mother had become mainstream, Mags was made to feel ashamed. She was a teenager and given no choice. It was too late to get rid of it, so she was shipped off to Aunt Alice's in Auckland, where 'that sort of thing' didn't unsettle the neighbours.

After she was born, she got to hold her once, and only because a nurse hadn't realised that she was being adopted. She brought her into the room and popped her into Mags arms, then left.

Thinking about it now, Mags could still feel her prickly red hair against her arms. Her face, so tiny, eyes closed and her fingers in her mouth as she sucked loudly on them. She was a good baby, quiet, with tiny hands clenching and unclenching, little feet and toes so soft and perfect. She had no more than ten minutes with her when the sister in charge stormed into the room with the nurse and whipped her away. A quarter of an hour later, Aunt Alice picked her up and took her back to the house, never to look back.

Mags came back from her thoughts and heard Aunt Barbara speaking. As usual she was reminiscing of an event in her life, this time of a lost love, and Mags though this was her way of showing some understanding for what she'd been through.

But Mags had never really loved the boy who fathered her child. They had been kids, and rivals at school, friends who didn't really fit in with the rest of the class.

They'd just been fooling around and things had got out of control. She stopped herself and concentrated on Aunt Barbara's voice, knowing that it would only distress her to think about it anymore.

There was a pause, and Aunt Barbara was looking kindly at her.

"I was 16, we were kids, and it was …" she too a breath, "it was for the best,"

"Did you ever wonder what happened?" she asked. Mags couldn't answer, her throat was tight, and she was trying hard not to cry. She nodded.

"I have the details of the adoption agency. They have opened their files on all 20th century adoptions. You can look for the child." Aunt Barbara spoke with an enthusiasm that Mags didn't feel. "That is, if you want to," she added looking at the lowered eyes and tight lip of Mags.

Filling up their glasses for one more time, Aunt Barbara took an envelope out of her pocket.

"It's my Christmas present to you," she said, "open it when you want. But if you should want to follow up on searching for the child, you have my support and any help I can give you."

Taking the envelop from her aunt, Mags was overwhelmed by her kindness and hugged the elderly woman.

"Thank you," she whispered, "I just don't know …"

"Hush now." Aunt Barbara held Mags shoulders and looked at her, "everyone has something they did at the time for all the right reasons. You now have a choice, to see the outcome of that decision or not. At least you get the chance, others … they will never know."

The woman looked out into the room; her eyes glazed over as she was lost in her own memories. She turned back to Mags. "In your own time, if or when you are ready."

They sat in silence sipping the Irish cream. The Christmas tree appeared to shine in the corner catching the evening light and radiated sparkles around the room.

Outside in the warm sunny evening they heard a truck turn into the street and the sounds of Christmas carols played by a brass band. The truck stopped further along from the cottage, and the two women decided they would go and listen closer.

Joined by other residents in the area, Mags found she was happy to sing along with the old favourite carols while a couple of helpers collected for the local food bank.

The next day Mags woke feeling optimistic about the future. While Aunt Barbara had her shower, Mags set the table with their Christmas Eve brunch of blueberry waffles with fruit comport, fresh brewed coffee and cheese scones that Bob had brought that morning, fresh from the oven. Bob didn't stay, he was doing his best to avoid Barbara, at Mags request, she didn't want any awkward questions from her aunt.

At 11 am, it was time for Aunt Barbara to go, she was packed up and with her gift from Mags safely tucked in her bag to be opened on Christmas day, she loaded up her car. Before leaving she gave Mags a big hug.

"Keep strong, Magnolia."

"I will, Aunt Barbara. Merry Christmas."

"You have a happy Christmas too, and take care," she replied, handing Mags a note. "If you want to talk, my cellphone number. And I've told my cousin you might ring. Like I said, they have plenty of room and they would squeeze you in, no question about it."

"I'll keep that in mind," replied Mags.

She climbed into the car, backed out of the driveway and drove down the road with a parting toot. Once she'd turned the corner, Mags opened the note to read what pearl of wisdom she had left this time. Her eyes grew wide and her mouth fell open, as the words leapt up at her from the paper.

"Is it all clear?' asked a voice from the street.

Mags turned and saw Bob standing by the garden gate. She nodded.

"What's the matter? You look pale, come inside and sit down." Bob ushered Mags into the sunroom at the back of the house, that she had used as a bedroom for the past few days. He got her to sit on the bed.

"It's Aunt Barbara," she said, Bob nodded, "she left me a note." Mags held a piece of white paper in her hands folded over so he couldn't see what was written on it.

"Ahha," said Bob, waiting for Mags to explain.

"She knows, she knows about us!" Mags looked at Bob a worried look on her face.

"Is that a bad thing?" he asked gently. Mags looked down at the paper again and shook her head.

"She seems happy for me, so I guess she approves."

"Wonderful, now I need to get you to the shop. There is that matter of the little party for the staff and knitters. I've got a great selection of treats, for the customers and our little party."

With everything that had been going on, Mags had forgotten all about it. But this would be a welcome distraction. She gathered her things up and walked along the street to where Bob had left the car, supposedly inconspicuous to all but the sharp-eyed Aunt Barbara. Trying to hide their friendship from her had been a definite failure.

On the trip to the shop Mags head was spinning, but today was not a day to stop and think, today was a day to be with friends and loved ones.

Christmas Day

"Seeing is believing, but sometimes the most real things in the world are the things we can't see."

— The Polar Express

Molly Sykes

It was bedlam in the Sykes household. Overnight the police arrived twice, once just before midnight and then again around 3 am, bringing with them temporary foster children for their care. This time of year, with stress and unrealistic expectations, could bring out the worst in some families. Not enough money for gifts and food, let alone a few extras for entertainment or need, caused some adults to tip over the edge. The ones caught in the middle were the children and Molly and her husband were prepared as they were every year.

First there was eleven-year-old Tash and ten-year-old Dexter, they'd been at the Sykes place before, and Tash was pleased 'her' bed wasn't in use. Tash, as usual was covered with bruises, had a split lip, and grazed knuckles. 'A feisty firebrand, defending her little brother or her mother,' thought Molly. Their social worker showed up not long after and wanted Tash to go to the hospital to check she was ok, but Tash was refusing to go and Ms. Rewai eventually gave in, as Tash let her clean the cuts with disinfectant and take photos for the record.

It was Dexter that Molly was worried about, the child was just skin and bone and seemed disconnected with reality.

If Tash went out of his sight he would start trembling, and Molly knew from past experience what would happen to this child if he was separated from his sister. It was the middle of the night, all she wanted to do was get these kids cleaned up and into a warm bed where they would be safe for the time being.

It was a habit of Molly's to keep some of the things her regulars had left behind on their last stay. She'd created a special box for each child. Once Ms. Rewai was finished with Tash, she had a quick word with Molly.

"Do you need anything?" she asked. Molly's brows knitted together.

"We're good. We've got some supplies from Foster Hope, and local charity donations" said Mr. Sykes returning to the kitchen where the children were eating chicken noodle soup and toast. "I've finished making up the beds in the third room," he said, 'it's ready when they are."

Ms. Rewai's phone rang, she sighed and answered it.

Molly put the boxes she'd kept for Tash and Dexter on the table. They looked at them with surprise as they recognised their names. Tash opened the box and let out a cry of joy. There was a Barbie doll with a blue glittery dress and a small plastic bag of other Barbie clothes. A book, a notebook with a unicorn on it and a pen with a unicorn rubber. Tears welled up in her eyes as she took out the Barbie and hugged her.

Dexter looked at Tash, he was alarmed as tears ran down her cheeks until she reassured him they were happy tears because they were safe.

She helped him take the lid off the dark blue box with glittery silver stars. Inside was a well-loved, almost threadbare teddy bear, with a new blue bow around his neck.

Tash took the bear out and handed it to Dexter he didn't want to take it at first. It took a while for him to recognize his bear, and suddenly his face lit up and he grabbed the bear from his sister's hand.

"Mine" he said.

"That's right Dex, he's yours, and the books in this box. Do you remember?"

Tash took the two picture books and one chapter book from the box along with a colouring book and crayons. He looked at them suspiciously and shook his head. Tash's face screwed up and she looked at Molly for help.

"That's ok. Dexter, you probably don't remember because it's late and you must be very tired." Molly looked at Dexter who nodded and then Tash who shrugged.

"I have to go," Ms. Rewai said to the children, "You'll stay with Mr. and Mrs. Sykes for a couple of days and then we'll know more about what's happening." She and Molly walked to the door and Molly handed her some mini fruit mince pies wrapped up in cellophane.

"Thank you for the coffee and these pies, it's going to be a long night. That was the police, another incident with more of my clients. God, I hate this time of year. It should be banned!" and with that she went out into the cloudy night to meet up with the police in another town.

Once the children had finished their supper, Molly handed over a new summer nighty for Tash and a pair of summer pajamas for Dexter. Each were given a pack of new underwear, facecloth and towel, a toothbrush, and a comb. They had arrived with only the clothes they stood up in. Once the children were safely tucked in bed and Mr. Sykes was reading them a goodnight story, Molly put their clothes in the wash. The hall cupboard had a selection of clothes collected over the years and she picked out shorts and t-shirts for both children that they could wear in the morning.

Molly and her husband had just got to sleep when the phone rang again, the police were bringing another, this time it was a baby. An hour later, Molly and her husband were holding a tiny baby, she looked like a newborn, but the police had no information about her. All they could say was that when the social worker arrived, they would be able to answer any questions.

Almost half an hour went by and no social worker. Molly wondered whether she should just settle the child down for the night but something about the child was not right and she had started to worry. She decided in the end to open a sachet of newborn formula they'd picked up from the chemist in preparation for the Christmas week.

It became apparent while trying to get the child to feed, there was something terribly wrong. The child was not interested in food and try as she might, she couldn't get the baby to take a bottle.

Where was that social worker?

Molly took her husband's hand and looked at him, while she cradled the baby. He knew that look.

This would not be the first time that a baby arrived on their doorstep beyond their ability to save it.

"Shall I go to the hospital?" he asked. Molly thought for a minute and then nodded.

"I'll have to stay here, the other's need me, I would leave Nicki and Ford with Lou but not with the new ones." Molly was torn, sometimes it was just too hard, and she felt inadequate. Her husband understood, he leant over and kissed her gently, taking the baby from her arms.

A knock at the door startled them. Molly went and opened the door to see a woman standing there with a girl of about 13 or 14.

"I'm Megan, social worker for Emma here, can we come in?" Molly let them in as they sat at the kitchen table, she poured Megan a milky coffee from the never-ending coffee pot she had on the go.

"Thank you, I needed that." she said after taking a gulp, "I haven't had a break since four this afternoon," she continued. She looked exhausted. "Is it always like this?"

"You must be new," chuckled Mr. Sykes, still holding the infant.

"Unfortunately, yes," replied Molly. "We are 'the last stop', emergency careers, so if you are here tonight, it's been a bad night." Megan's eyes grew wide and all she could say was 'Oh!'

"We're worried about the baby." said Mr. Sykes, "She won't take the bottle, she hasn't made a sound and she's so tiny. It's hard to keep her warm, even on this humid night. I was just about to take her to the hospital."

"That's why I'm here," explained Megan. "I was late cause … well I'm here now." She signed and gave an exhausted smile.

"We'll take the baby to the hospital; we have a baby seat in the car. Is that infant formula?"

"Newborn formula, yes. The police couldn't give us any information, so we went with our gut feeling."

"Good move, she's only hours old." Megan looked to Emma who had said nothing the entire time. She was looking at Mr. Sykes holding the baby. Molly was struck with an idea.

"Right, you need baby clothes and another blanket. Emma, would you like to come with me and pick something from our spares, and let Megan finish her coffee?" The girl looked up her brown eyes wide, her bottom lip trembled, and she looked to Megan for support.

"It's alright" said Megan and she smiled at Emma and gave a little nod.

The bottom shelf of the hall cupboard had packets of disposable nappies, pre-loved grow suits, and some little knitted cardigans from the knitting groups along with new baby blankets still wrapped. Molly handed Emma a packet of nappies for newborns, a handful of formular sachets and a spare bottle. She then got her to choose a blanket for the baby. The young teen sat down on the floor and picked out a super soft pink elephant cuddle blanket along with two newborn grow suits. One with feet in pink and red stripes and the other without feet and animal prints. She also chose a pale green cardigan and Molly handed over two singlets, a gauze face cloth and baby towel. For the first time Emma looked alive and Molly just knew that this young girl had to suddenly become an adult. Her heart ached for her.

"I'll put these in a backpack for you, then you've got your hands free," said Molly pulling out a new pink and purple backpack from the top of the cupboard.

"Oh, is this for me?" she asked. Molly nodded. "Thank you. I've never had a new backpack before." Molly smiled at her, she was glad to bring some joy in the girl's life even if it were only for a minute or two.

The baby bottle with formula was sitting on the kitchen table, a bad sign, the baby still hadn't had anything to eat. Molly added a box of disinfectant tables for the bottles into the backpack. They were now ready for the hospital.

"Here's my card," said Megan, in case you need me.

"And here's ours, in case you need us," said Mr. Sykes. "We have room for Emma and the baby, but just give us a warning you're on your way." Megan took the card and nodded. Mr. Sykes handed the baby to Emma who almost dropped it, until he showed her how to cradle her. She seemed terrified but she carefully followed Megan out to the car and put the baby into the car seat as instructed by Mr. Sykes, while Megan phoned the Masterton hospital to tell them they were on their way.

Waving goodbye as the car went down the street, Mr. Sykes put his arms around his wife. "I think we'll see those two again," he said, and she nodded.

"Bed, we need some sleep. Ford may not know much about Christmas, but Nicki does, and I'll bet she's up at dawn. Shall we put the stockings for them in their rooms so it will keep them occupied?"

Molly was tired, this would keep them in their rooms for a bit she thought but Mr. Sykes shook his head.

"A book from Santa, that's all," he replied. "You know how much you enjoy watching them on Christmas day, we don't want to miss that do we?" Molly smiled; he was right. In the kitchen she checked the coffee pot, it would stay on for another half an hour. Everything was turned off, wrapped books from Santa were left at the bottom of the beds for all 5 in their care, and then Molly and her husband climbed into bed for the second time that night. It was around 4.30 am when they drifted off to sleep.

***

It was coming up to 8 am when Nicki woke up. Ford was still asleep but her joy at finding a present at the end of her bed had her squealing and jumping up and down which woke him up. He cowered under the blanket at the noise.

Carefully he peeked out to see Nicki flicking through a book with colourful pictures, it looked like there were lots of words and Ford shuddered. He hated reading because he found it difficult. The parcel at the end of his bed looked suspiciously like Nicki's. He didn't know much about Christmas; he was shunted from place to place all the time and he couldn't even remember where he was this time last year.

Nicki sat on the edge of his bed and showed him the pictures. "Do you know these stories?' she asked. He shook his head.

"Can you read them?" he asked. Nicki gave him a hug and climbed onto the bed, so they sat side by side with their backs against the wall. The book was of fairy stories, myths, and legends from around the world and Nicki was in her element reading aloud as Ford listened and looked at the pictures.

Molly woke up at 8.20 am and listened intently for the noise of children in the house. There was nothing, and she breathed a sigh of relief. A quick shower and she was ready for the day before her husband had even woken up. It had been a miracle that there had been no more middle of the night emergencies, and she picked up her check list for the day and made some adjustments.

She was in the kitchen making a fresh pot of coffee and a batch of her special Christmas morning muffins was in the oven when the phone rang. It was Megan from the hospital giving her an update.

The fresh coffee and smell of fruity muffins piled high in a basket on the kitchen table brought Lou out of her room, already dressed. She sat at the table and took one of the muffins, smothering it with butter.

"These are wonderful," she said, "are they special?"

"Of course, for Christmas," replied Molly. "Did you find your present?" she asked.

"Was that at the foot of my bed, it just said From Santa, I didn't know what it was, so I left it." Molly nodded; how could she have forgotten to add 'For Lou' on the label? Before she could say anything, Mr. Sykes entered the kitchen.

"Is that Mrs. Sykes' world famous in New Zealand Christmas muffins I smell?" he asked.

Molly smiled and handed him his coffee as he gave her a good morning kiss.

"I think I'd better go and see what the others are up to," said Molly. "Let Lou know about our new guests will you dear?"

Molly gave a light tap on the door of Nicki and Fords room, and when she opened it, she was pleased to see Ford so engrossed in the stories that he didn't tremble in fear as she entered the room. She waited until Nicki had finished the chapter before telling them to come to the kitchen for breakfast. As they left, Molly noticed Ford hadn't opened his present from Santa. She left it where it was and closed the door following the children into the hall.

The other spare room was in the other corridor from the kitchen and Molly tapped on the door of room with Tash and Dexter.

They were both up and had been going through the clothes Molly had left for them to try. They had unwrapped the presents on the bed, and Dexter was reading his 'pick your own path' story while Tash just turned the book over in her hand, looking at it with disdain. They dropped the books and stood to attention when Molly entered the room.

"Those books are for you," she said, and Ford smiled picking up his book and looking for the page he'd been on. Tash looked at the book lying on the ground as if it were offensive.

"Come and have breakfast, there are some Christmas morning muffins, but you can have anything you want, if we have it of course," chuckled Molly.

"Come and meet Nicki, Ford and Lou, they are looking forward to meeting you."

Neither child smiled as both left the room with serious looks on their faces as they went to meet the other housemates. Molly followed them into the kitchen she knew the day would be difficult, but she was determined to make it as pleasant as she could for all of them.

"Santa Claus is anyone who loves another and seeks to make them happy; who gives himself by thought or word or deed in every gift that he bestows."

- Edwin Osgood Grover

Sir Neville Emerson

The house was quiet. Sir Neville wandered into the kitchen, wearing his pajamas and a dressing gown, expecting to have to make instant coffee. He found the coffee pot in the process of filling with the rich dark liquid. He looked around for Edith, his housekeeper, expecting to see her standing at the sink, but no one was there. Edith, he thought as he remembered their conversation the day before, was insistent on setting the timer for the morning. He chuckled, but he appreciated having his usual coffee waiting when he got up.

It was Christmas day and he insisted all his household staff have the day off, and reassured them that they were welcome to invite family to their houses on the estate and wander the gardens if they were so inclined.

It was usually dictated by the weather. The last few Christmases had been disappointing with rain, clouds, and mist. Today looked no different. Clouds blocked what should have been a bright day as he looked out to the rose garden from his bedroom that morning before coming downstairs.

The view from the kitchen was the same, where the rustling of the willows by the water race should have had morning light playing over the surfaces of the kitchen, there was just dull nothing. 'Maybe it will get better later,' he thought. A delicious smell caused his stomach to rumble.

It was just like Edith to have made a batch of cheese scones this morning and left some for him to find. Next to the coffee machine was a plate with three plump, fresh scones covered with a napkin and a little present wrapped in silver paper with a green bow. He smiled and hoped she and her husband had found their present. He'd smuggled it into their back yard a couple of days ago – covered it with a tarpaulin and told them there was a problem with the pipes. He, Sarah and Julie got the tarpaulin off around midnight, hoping Edith and her husband were heavy sleepers.

The present was an intricate wrought iron benched ornamental arbor along with a couple of books by their favourite authors. Their old park bench had seen better days and the wood had rotted over winter. With Sarah's guidance, they'd found Edith's favourite roses and climbing plants. With the arbor, they had shelter from the sun and there would be no need to get back inside in the afternoons when the sun was at its peak. As much as he hated to hear it, he knew they were all getting older, and it was near time to hang up the business suit, or in Edith's case, the apron, and to enjoy the late afternoon and evening of life.

He poured himself a coffee then leaned against the bench thinking of the day ahead. Picking out one of the scones he ate silently while looking out the window.

He sighed as he finished the scone and sipped his drink. He never got sick of looking out into the kitchen garden and beyond but he was starting to wonder how many years he had left to enjoy it.

"Stop that," he told himself. "Only positive thoughts." He finished his coffee in silence, watching morning rays peep through the clouds and play on the leaves creating many shades of green. 'If only the weather would only come to the party and fine up later today, we could use the sun to brighten our days,' he thought.

The coffee cup slipped from his hand, and it shattered on the linoleum floor.

"Damn and blast!" He flexed his fingers and found it difficult, he rubbed his hand, the pins and needles were back. A scowl crossed his face as he collected a brush and pan from the broom closet to clean up the mess. 'Not now,' he pleaded to himself, 'not today.'

The Santa costume was laid out in his dressing room, along with a packed carry-all containing a change of clothes. In the hall, a sack filled with presents sat waiting to be loaded into the car, several people had donated items for gifts, and with Sarah, Bob and Molly's help, he hoped he had enough for everyone who showed up today.

All he had to do was get into costume and arrive on time. He climbed the stairs slowly, today was a bad day. In his room he sat on his bed and opened the draw of the bedside table, pulled out a folder and checked the contents. The papers were all in order. Closing the folder and putting it in an envelope he added it to the carry-all. Was he ready for this? He didn't know, but today was a good reminder that changes happen, and he needed to do them on his terms.

He'd see Sarah later; she'd be at the Hog and Frog to help at the main event. As he thought about her, he smiled and wondered how she would react to the surprise he had for her.

Nettie Sanderson

It was a cool misty morning when Nettie awoke, head butted by Prissy who was having histrionics over an empty food dish. The alarm clock showed it was just after 8 am. Nettie threw off the bed covers and got out of bed. How could she have slept in? Why hadn't the alarm gone off at the usual 7 am.

Quickly showering and dressing, she grabbed her handbag and headed for the kitchen to feed Prissy before going to the shop. She'd just found her keys, not in their usual place for some strange reason, and she was about to walk out the front door when she heard her neighbour Sam calling out Merry Christmas. She stopped in her tracks it dawned on her.

Walking back to the kitchen to put the filter coffee pot on, Nettie couldn't believe she'd forgotten it was Christmas day. At least she was dressed, as she remembered there was a planned Skype call with Ryan at 9.30 am. She hoped the present for Greena had arrived in time and was looking forward to seeing her son and granddaughter.

A knock on her patio door made her turn, and she saw her neighbour Sam sporting a colourful Christmas outfit with a Santa hat. She unlocked the door to let him in.

"Coffee?" she asked "It's a fresh pot."

"Love one," replied Sam and before he took another step had Prissy purring around his legs.

"Hello Ms. Chicken Thief," he said chortling. Nettie grimaced at the memory of Prissy bringing a half chicken home. The pugnacious cat had helped herself to the Sloan's dinner while it was thawing on a bench. Nettie didn't know Prissy wandered to the Sloan's place, two doors down from Sam until she searched for the rightful owners of the chicken. Nettie had apologised several times, replaced the chicken, and brought the Sloan's a bottle of wine and Christmas treats from Schoc Chocolates in Greytown, but they still seemed angry about it.

Sam noticed the look on Nettie's face and laughed, as he sat at the kitchen table. Handing him his coffee, Nettie looked at her neighbour with her head tipped to one side, and wondered why he was laughing at her.

"The Sloan's eh," said Sam. "Couldn't have picked a worse couple to upset," he chuckled again and leaned over to pat Prissy who was still treating him as a long-lost best friend. "They are the original curmudgeonly couple. Doesn't matter what you do, it'll be wrong, or it will have upset them in some way that they feel obliged to tell you about it. I'm often on the other end of a tongue lashing. She's a real 'Karen', with an annoyingly shrill voice, and far worse than he is. He'll just mumble passive aggressively at you."

"I have to say I never had anything to do with them, until now."

"I'd say those days are over. You'll probably hear from them more than you want to. They seem to find fault with everything. The lights are too bright at your house, you are making too much noise. They even come and tell me when I should be mowing my lawn."

"Goodness!" Nettie had never heard anything like it. "Are there really people like that?"

"Afraid so. But don't worry, you won't be the only one they pick on and you won't be the last. Welcome to the club," Sam laughed again. "There's a group of us that meet up at the pub just to vent about the latest things the Sloan's are outraged over. They are aghast at everything."

"Retired couple?" asked Nettie. If they were recently retired, and didn't know what to do with their time, that could explain it.

"No, that's the thing, they are probably only in their 50's. He's got a job in Lower Hutt, commutes every day, and she has work in an office or something in Masterton. How they find the time to complain about everything I'll never know. But you're in luck. They are away for Christmas, so we can breathe easy for a couple of days." Sam let out another laugh. Nettie was pleased to see her once shy and pedantic neighbour was now relaxed and happy in her company.

"Just a little Christmas gift for you," said Sam handing over a beautifully wrapped gift, a box about the size of a coaster. Nettie's eyes widened, and a smile crossed her face as she thanked him.

Excusing herself for a minute, she went to the lounge where a small pile of presents sat under a small artificial tree, her only attempt at decorating this year.

She picked up a soft bulky parcel and took it back to the kitchen.

"For you," she said handing it to Sam, "Merry Christmas."

They drank coffee and opened their gifts; Sam was thrilled with his olive-coloured summer jersey made of cotton and knitted by Nettie. He put it on immediately and Nettie was relieved it was a perfect fit.

When Nettie opened her gift, she gasped. It was a beautifully crafted set of key rings with a metal silver finish, and different colours enameled to show wool skeins. It was a key ring decorated with a wool stash. Sam explained he had a friend that made bespoke jewelry and he'd helped design it, just for her. It was one of the most thoughtful gifts she'd ever received. Her late husband, Alex, had never managed to get her gifts right, and once the children were older, she had given them the task of supervising their father's gift shopping. But the result was that Ryan was as good as his father, and Vanessa always got voted down. This gift from Sam restored her faith that men could give fantastic gifts.

Finishing his coffee, Sam stood to leave, but was almost tripped by Prissy becoming entangled in his feet.

"I don't have any family so I'm going to the lunch at the Hog and Frog. How about you? Do you have family coming today?"

"No, they're all doing their own thing this year," said Nettie with a sigh. She hadn't really thought much about what she was doing today, the shop had taken up all her time.

"My friend and previous neighbour, Beth, is arriving this morning, but it was last minute, and I don't have anything special planned for lunch, so I had been thinking of going, but I wasn't sure if both of us should go to the Hog and Frog."

"Nonsense, it'll be fine." said Sam. "Then it's settled, we're doing to this party together. The three of us. I'm pleased you're going. I don't really know who will be there, but if we put our glad rags on, we can make an entrance." Nettie nodded, she agreed, turning up to events on your own always took an extra bit of courage.

"Ok, you've talked me into it," she said with a smile.

Waving goodbye to Sam as he slipped through the gate back to his house, Nettie was pleased he was her neighbour. Just then her phone chimed with a text. It was time to Skype the family.

*"Nothing ever seems too bad, too hard, or too sad
when you've got a Christmas tree in the living
room."*

- Nora Roberts

Mags Wild

The wind rustled the back porch door waking Mags from a deep sleep. She shivered and pulled a banket close around her, wondering where the rest of them had got to. She looked down on the floor to find the blankets in a heap, not for the first time.

The Christmas eve get together in the shop went on quite late and when she got home, the thought of making her bed after Aunt Barbara's visit was too hard. It was easier to crawl back into the spare bed in the sunroom at the back of the house and sort everything out in the morning.

It was dull and slightly blustery, and at 8 am it was still nippy. Sitting up, Mags found her slippers and dressing gown and walked into the house to make breakfast.

While waiting for the kettle to boil she went through her carry all siting on the kitchen table. A few of them had exchanged gifts and she looked at the carefully wrapped parcels, still unopened.

As she had a tree, the presents should sit under that and she carried them into the sitting room. There was a total of six and it really did look perfect having the parcels there.

It was then she noticed the envelope from Aunt Barbara sitting on the mantel, and a feeling of dread overwhelmed her for a second. Looking back down at the parcels a smile played on her lips, she'd open them after breakfast.

The coffee plunger was full and as a treat Mags had decided to make herself French toast for breakfast. The thought of the fried eggy delight with cinnamon sugar made her feel like it really was Christmas day. Her grandmother would make French toast on special days and Mags became quite nostalgic for times when she was young and carefree. As the toast fried, she added a few strawberries to the plate and poured herself a coffee.

This was one of the joys of living alone, Mags decided, you could eat what you wanted, when you wanted it and in the case of today, savour every mouthful in peace. As she chewed, she thought of the present in the envelope. Well, it was more like the envelope kept intruding into her thoughts. Did she want to know? Why stir things up now, it had been a long time ago and too much had happened. She took a sip of coffee and then another bite.

'What if she doesn't want to see me?' she thought. 'Even worse, she could hate me.' She was becoming distracted and most of the breakfast had gone. She decided to concentrate on what she was doing and think about the envelope later.

After breakfast the presents were opened, and marvelled at; a couple were beautiful, some were tricky and all were very thoughtful. Mags got up and filled her coffee cup. Walking back into the sitting room, she glared at the envelope.

In a sudden flourish, Mags opened it before she could second guess herself, unfolding the papers inside. There it was, the Pandora's box was open, no turning back now.

There in her hands was a birth certificate for the baby girl from so long ago. Mags had called her Poppy; she was an ANZAC baby born in April. There were more documents in the letter than Mags had imagined, including the letters of adoption and the name the child had been raised under. She felt disappointing her new parents hadn't used the name Poppy, but they made that decision and there was nothing she could do about it.

Taking a gulp of coffee, Mags realised it had gone cold and was about to make more when her phone chimed. A text from Bob asking what time she was going to the Hog and Frog. Her face screwed up as she wondered what he was on about. Then she remembered, they were going to the Hog and Frog for Christmas lunch, otherwise they both would be spending the day alone. Bob had offered to make some treats for Sir Neville; she remembered the conversation now. But surely there would be some of his family or friends visiting later, so she replied she still hadn't decided.

Within minutes, the phone rang. It was Bob, convincing her to come to the lunch. No, all his family were busy elsewhere and he was looking forward to meeting at the Hog and Frog. He was going to pick her up because the weather was changeable. Mags gave in and with a sigh, got in the shower while wondering what to wear.

***

"Thanks Bob," said Mark as he brought through plates of baked cookies and treats to go on the buffet table for lunch. "You know Sir Neville had caterers dropping off the food this morning, so there is plenty.

"Did they also deliver plates of treats and cardboard containers to take home?" asked Bob. Mark nodded as they walked through into the kitchen. "Then these," he held out a bag of fudge pieces wrapped in clear bags tied with colourful ribbons, "can be added to them. The rest are for people to help themselves with coffee."

"You're a marvel Bob," said Mark admiring the amount of work that had gone into getting the two types of petit-fours and the fudge ready for the lunch.

"Leave them here and I'll make sure that Heather gets them out with the coffee."

"I didn't think there were staff on today," said Bob.

"Heather volunteered, and if Dan gets here for lunch, she volunteered him too," answered Mark with a guffaw. "I'm pretty sure it's going to be a big surprise when he gets here."

"How's Mandy?' asked Bob. Mags eyes widened, with everything going on, she'd forgotten about Mandy's ordeal.

"Tired, it's taking a toll. She would never have agreed to this if we hadn't convinced her that she need do nothing, and Sir Neville would have it all under control." Mark gave a little snort, "I have to supervise of course, she doesn't trust anyone to do it right, but I think with the people he employed, Heather and all the helpers, we've made a pretty good bash of it. She'll be down when it all starts."

Bob smiled and nodded, and Mags smiled at Mark. He really did love Mandy; it must be hard to see her going through radiation therapy and having to keep the hotel going. It was times like this that Mags realised that life could take a turn for the worst and it didn't matter whether you were with someone or if you lived alone.

As Bob and Mags helped set out food on trays, people started to arrive, and Sir Neville entered the kitchen dressed as Santa.

"Ho, Ho, Ho. Merry Christmas everyone!" Sir Neville was carrying a large bag and plopped it on the floor. "Do we have everything in order? Need any help there?"

"It's all under control," replied Mark, "Bob's made treats to go with coffee and fudge to go in the take home pack. We're just adding them in now before we lose track of what's been done and what hasn't."

"Thank you, Bob, I'm sure everyone will appreciate them." Sir Neville picked one of the petit-fours up and popped it in his mouth. "Delicious. You really are an excellent baker," he added. Mags was surprised to see a smile on Bob's face with a slight flush of red.

"And Mags, so wonderful to see you here today. How was the visit from your Aunt Barbara?" Sir Neville stooped forward to speak to Mags who was taken by surprise. She had no idea he knew anything about her aunt.

"She's well thank-you and just the same as always," she replied. Sir Neville let out a raucous laugh.

"That's what I thought too when I spoke with her. Used to serve, you know, she was tough then, and she hasn't changed a bit." Mags looked at Sir Neville, her eyes wide open. He gave her a wink.

"There you are," said Sarah looking over the Santa outfit as she walked into the kitchen from the dining room. You're supposed to be mingling and handing out punch. Come on, oh and put that sack under the tree."

"Yes Ma'am," replied Sir Neville and with a jolly laugh, he picked up the bag and walked out into the dining room to mingle with the locals who arrived earlier. It looked like the event would have a good attendance based on the number that had started to gather, he just hoped the tremor in his arm would disappear. He just needed to get through the day...

Beth Brookhurst

It was just another day for Beth, she got up half an hour later than her usual time and went into the kitchen to make coffee and feed Pepi and Ms. The Boss. The midnight Christmas service at St Andrews had been fun, even though she had been called in last minute to help out. It made her feel like part of the community and that she was still useful. There had been phone calls to Lizzy and Nettie to let them know she wouldn't be arriving in Thornbury until Christmas day.

Lizzie was going to Masterton for the day to spend the day with friends, and Beth had arranged to go straight to Netties house. Beth had been disappointed that neither Ryan nor Vanessa would be around this year. But Nettie assured her she would be welcome to join her at the pub lunch. Beth shook her head, lunch at the Hog and Frog didn't sound very Christmassy, and she almost said she wouldn't come over until Boxing Day, but Nettie seemed to be looking forward to it, and if Beth were honest, she was feeling a little lonely.

The way Nettie described the lunch made it sound as if it could be fun, she relented and agreed to drive over on Christmas morning.

Beth and the dogs would spend a few days at Nettie's, they'd have a back yard to roam around in but they would stay in the house while the women went to lunch.

While packing, Beth hoped she would meet some likeminded people. It had been a fortnight since she'd finished work, but every now and then she missed the company.

By 10.10 am the car was packed and the little dogs were in their carry cages and strapped into the back seat. The road was reasonably busy for a public holiday and pulling out on to State Highway 2 going towards the Wairarapa was almost as busy as a normal weekend.

The trip over the Remutaka Hill was slow, as travellers navigated the unfamiliar road. Not so many trucks, but camper vans and caravans with holiday makers made up for it. Usually an impatient driver, Beth took a sip of her water and switched the radio to the oldies station known as 'FM Magic', where they played the music of her youth. It wasn't long before she was singing along to a familiar song as she drove.

It was just after 11.30 am when Beth turned onto Nettie's driveway on Mayfair Way. Nettie was standing at the door as the car came to a halt, and came out to meet her dear friend. Between them they took Beth's bags to the spare room and the dogs were let out on the back lawn.

After a tentative start, both the dogs made the most of a run around the back garden, happy to be released from their carry cages.

When they were settled down and back in the house, Nettie called out to her neighbour that they were ready to walk down the road to the Hog and Frog. Sam was charming, chatting all the way and paid such interest to Beth that Nettie started to think they knew each other.

Normally Beth would have been standoffish and wonder what he was up to, but these few days away from the sometimes-toxic work environment had made her more relaxed and happier. Nettie looked over at her friend laughing at Sam's jokes and raised an eyebrow, it was rare to see her talking to a stranger like an old friend.

It was these little things, Beth decided, these small acts of kindness that gave her a lift. Beth was telling Sam about how the anticipation of meeting new people made her look like she was grumpy. Nettie almost fell over when she heard that, everyone who knew Beth was well aware that this was the way Beth was, but not one of them thought she knew that about herself.

They continued walking and chatting, and it was obvious that Beth felt safe with Sam and Nettie. 'I need to go out more,' thought Beth, as she realised that she would have to organise going to these types of events herself, hunt them out or maybe join a club. She listened to Sam talk about the latest adventures of Prissy the chicken thief, and wondered if such a club existed and if it did, what sort of things would they do.

"Nothing ever seems too bad, too hard, or too sad when you've got a Christmas tree in the living room."

- Nora Roberts

The Main Event

It wasn't long before Nettie, Sam and Beth arrived at the Hog and Frog, entering the colourfully decorated main entrance on Slip Street, with its bubble Christmas tree, wreath, and lights. Sam insisted on a selfie with the two women by the door,

"Just want to put some pics on my social media, let everyone know I'm having a wonderful time," he said. Nettie raised her eyebrows. Was the quiet, socially awkward man that lived next door to her gone for good? He certainly had come out of his shell and she'd been surprised at how much fun he was becoming.

Walking through into the dining room, the sight before them took their breath away. A large pine decorated in the same types and colours of bubbles as the outdoor tree, and under it were parcels wrapped in Christmas paper. Next to the tree was a large chair and there sat Santa, chatting to a couple of people. Others were mingling and getting settled at tables, catching up with friends.

Mark was carrying a tray of glasses, filled with options of bubbles or orange juice, while Heather and Bob were walking around with trays of nibbles.

Nettie was very impressed that Bob was doing a great job as a waiter, probably under the watchful eye of Mandy, thought Nettie.

She looked around, but Mandy was nowhere to be seen.

'In the kitchen, getting the food organised,' thought Nettie as she went over to Mark to help herself to a drink, she was followed by Beth and Sam.

A cheer rose from a group of people gathered nearby and Nettie looked around to see who had turned out for the day. Apart from Sam, Beth, and Bob, she saw Mags sitting over at a table talking to a woman Nettie didn't know. Sarah, Sir Neville's PA and her wife, Julie were at a table chatting to some older women. Derek, the handyman/gardener from the Hidden Woods Boutique Hotel was talking with a couple of men Nettie recognised as regulars in the pub, but she didn't know their names. She did hope that someone would keep an eye on the amount of alcohol Derek consumed. He was known to go on benders. Heather was still walking around with the nibbles and Ross had taken over Mark's drink tray.

At the back, at a table Nettie noticed Lou from the hair saloon next to her shop, she was with a young woman in a wheelchair, and another woman she didn't know. Scanning the rest of the room, there were some faces she recognised, some were people she'd talked to, others she'd just seen them in the street, and a few never seen before.

As 12.30 arrived, a hush fell over the dining room and from the back kitchen, Mandy entered. She was dressed all in silver with touches of green, Mark was on her arm and he was dressed in red and gold.

Nettie pressed her lips together, was he wearing that when she spoke with him just a few minutes ago?

She honestly couldn't remember, but it was Mandy who seemed to glow. She looked amazing.

They walked through the dining room, the silent guests parted making a path through the crowd, until they stood in front of the tree, next to Sir Neville who was standing and in his full Santa Claus regalia.

He was tall, and Nettie knew there was a handsome man under that white beard and padded suit. Her heart pounded as she remembered their encounter last year. She enjoyed talking to him and it was especially nice that he remembered everyone's name and what they had told him about themselves. He was a convivial host.

Sir Neville stepped forward. "Welcome, welcome one and all," he called out. Around the room there were smiles and excited chatter.

"So lovely to see so many faces, new friends and old, and a big thank you to Mark and Mandy Weatherby for indulging me, once again," he looked at Mandy and smiled, "to play Santa. It's the highlight of my year." There were a few oohs, and chuckles.

"The food is buffet, help yourself, it's in the bar and you can sit anywhere. We have the Hog and Frog to ourselves for the day, so grab a plate, enjoy your Christmas lunch and make new friends."

The noise of excited chatter grew as people drifted through the doors between the dining room and the bar. The sight before them was lavish. Ham on the bone, carved by Mark, chicken, potatoes, greens, salads with sauces and gravy. For some of the older townsfolk on fixed incomes, or who lived alone, this was as a feast of epic proportion.

As Sir Neville wandered around mingling and seeing to everyone's needs, he was greeted with handshakes, hugs and tears of happiness from grateful citizens.

Mark and Bob were following behind, checking people off on their lists, adding those they knew and chatting with those they didn't to find out their names. No one was going to miss out.

Nettie marvelled at the amount of work that would have gone into creating the lunch. She sat at a table with Beth and three others, people she hadn't met before, even so, she found it easy to chat. 'Good food and good wine made for good company,' she thought. Even Beth was enjoying herself, something she would never have done in previous years, preferring to be on her own for most of the day.

A call went out for seconds, and almost immediately there was a polite queue waiting for more.

"I'm going up for more," said Beth, 'that ham was the nicest I've ever had, and such a great selection of salads. What a treat this is, are you coming?" But before Nettie could answer, Beth was up and joining the back of the queue.

Then the deserts came out, set up on another table. Fruit salad, trifle, pavlova and ice cream, overseen by Heather. A variety of sweet and gooey sauces caught Nettie's eye. She knew that she'd probably have two helpings of desert to get all of what was on offer.

Standing in the queue for pavlova and ice cream, Nettie found herself next to Lou, the teen's face was lit up with such a delight that Nettie couldn't help but smiling with her.

"Isn't this great?" said Lou quietly to Nettie.

"Mrs Sykes said it would be, but I wasn't going to come because I couldn't imagine what it would be like."

"She said I'd miss out on a wonderful experience and she'd put me to work minding the new kids if I didn't. She even got Nurse Kipps to pick me up on her way. I'm so very glad, she did. All this food, and all these people. It's wonderful." Nettie agreed totally as she wondered who Nurse Kipps was. "I've never had a Christmas like this before. Do you do this every year?"

"This is my first time at Sir Neville's Christmas day lunch." replied Nettie, "Usually I have my family stay with me or I go to them, but this year was a little different and here I am with my friend Beth from the Hutt. She's staying for a couple of days but she only arrived this morning."

"Oh, you have something like this with your family?" Lou asked.

"Not so grand, but yes. The tree and decorations, the lunch, the presents, everything," replied Nettie.

"Presents? Are there presents?" Lou asked her eyes wide with surprise.

"Definitely presents, you'll see. I'd say they'll be after lunch back in the dining room. Did you see them all under the tree?"

"I thought they were just decorations" replied Lou, her eyes still wide as she tried to keep her excitement under control. "Like the ones in shop windows. I didn't know that people got presents."

Before Nettie could reply Heather was standing holding out a piece of pavlova and asking what flavoured ice cream she wanted. They then parted and she didn't get a chance to speak to Lou again.

The initial loud chatter was once again subdued as people finished their meals and sat back in seats, unfastening belt buckles and taking off jackets and cardigans. Looks of satisfaction showed that everyone had ample sufficiency and probably would be happy for a nap, but it was time to go back into the dining room while Santa's elves cleaned up.

They walked into the room; chairs had been set up so no one had to stand. Santa, Mark and Mandy were by the tree. Tea and coffee were being served at the bar, Ross and Dan were walking around with a tray of Christmas cake while Bob passed around a tray with his petite fours that no one refused. 'No matter how full you are,' thought Nettie, 'there is always room for Christmas cake and sweet treats.'

"While everyone gets a cuppa and some cake, let's have a few Christmas carols," boomed Sir Neville, and right on queue music started up and a small group from the local little theatre group appeared, singing 'Jingle Bell's' and inviting the audience to join in. She saw the usual line up from the theatre group with one new addition. Sam was there, dressed as an elf, his long thin legs in candy cane striped tights with a green thigh length tunic and an elf hat with elf ears attached. Suppressing a smile, she marvelled again at how far her quiet neighbour had come.

Two more songs and a rousing rendition of 'We wish you a Merry Christmas' saw the Christmas themed singers go back into the audience. Nettie turned around in her seat and found Sam sitting with a couple of fellow thespians.

A movement at the very back of the room caught her eye and she saw Molly Sykes standing by the door, holding the hand of a young girl that Nettie thought would have been about seven or eight.

"It wouldn't be Christmas without a gift, how about some presents?" called Santa to the room.

A cheer went up and the chatter of anticipation started as the first names were called out. By the tree, Sarah was picking up parcels and handing them to Mandy, who then whispered the recipient's name as she handing them to Santa. Mark stood next to the chair, checking names off on a clip board, it was his job to make sure no one missed out. There were squeals of delight, laughter and light chatter. Santa had a friendly word with everyone and happily posed for selfies.

Almost half the presents had been given out when Santa stood up and stretched. "I have the first of some special moments," he said. Mandy was smiling and handed a large box to him. "For most of us, this is a day with memories, good and bad, of Christmas's past and a day to feel the love of family and friends. But for one of us here, there are no memories, and this is the first of what we hope are many happy memories. A young woman who has been through a bit of an ordeal lately and we want her to know, that this is a happy time, no matter what your faith, we don't care at this event, it's for everyone." A few hear, hears went up from those assembled.

"Louise, come and get your first gift from Santa."

"For Me?" said Lou, as she tentatively walked toward Santa, her face flushed, eyes wide and her mouth slightly apart. The young woman took the package and the smile on her face made everyone happy.

"A photo of this momentous occasion," said Mark, "Lou, you stand next to Santa, that's it, say Christmas Cheer!" Mark took about four photos, just to be safe, before letting Lou back to her seat.

On her way she ripped the paper off the parcel and stopped in her tracks. Inside the box was the latest android phone, brand new. She turned and looked back at Sir Neville; he was watching her.

"For me?' she mouthed at him. A smile crossed his lips as he nodded, before going back to concentrating on the next gift recipient. There was much more and Lou sat down looking at each item, carefully chosen just for her. Tears welled in her eyes and she was comforted by the two women at the table and Molly who came and put her hand on Lou's shoulder.

More names were called out including Beth, who wasn't going to go up until Nettie explained it had been organised for her to get a gift. Then Nettie, she received a lovely scarf in autumnal colours made from hand died silk accordion to the label. She recognised it from being the same local supplier that Nancy Scott stocked, and was immediately impressed by the thoughtfulness of the gift. Beth received a small painting and Nettie recognised the signature immediately. It was one of Bron's artworks. Nettie wasn't sure what Beth would think of it, but there was nothing to worry about as Beth loved her gift.

Well over half had received their gifts, but Nettie noticed Mags hadn't been up yet. Looking around, she saw her shop manager sitting on her own, away from others and looking at the young woman in the wheel chair as if she'd never seen anything like it.

"And another special occasion." Santa's loud voice drowned those that were so busing chatting and caused Nettie to turn. "A well-known character of our town, that has been helping me out with a special project. She also has a special birthday coming up that I wanted to acknowledge. Mags Wild. Will you join me at the front?" It wasn't really a question but an order. The sort you become expert at when you've spent time in the forces.

A slight scowl crossed Mags's face, she didn't like being the centre of attention and then decided it would only be a minute or two if she got it over and done with and didn't dilly dally. Her strawberry red hair shone almost copper and gold from the afternoon sun coming in from the skylight, as she picked her way past the chairs on her way to the front. The short stature of Mags next to the towering Sir Neville was quite a contrast. Santa handed Mags her present and insisted they stop for a photo. Mark had to have several goes while he tried to get Mags to smile, in the end he gave up and settled for a non-scowl.

"From your Aunt Barbara, she insisted," whispered Sir Neville with a smile. It seemed that Mags couldn't get back to her seat quick enough.

It was the next gift, when Santa stood again. Everyone turned as a woman pushed the wheelchair forward in anticipation. Sir Neville smiled at the two women, their backs to the audience.

"This is a special treat for us today. It's one of those Christmas miracles that you hear about that fuel the plot of hundreds of Christmas movies and feel-good novels." Sir Neville cleared his throat. This was harder than he thought.

"A young girl has endeared herself into the hearts of several of our residents," Nettie noticed Bob and a couple of other people come forward to stand next to the wheelchair. 'This is fascinating, what's going on?' she wondered.

"She came to Thornbury amid a tragedy, but with such a positive attitude, never taking no for an answer. She has helped more people than she realises. It is now time for us to give back," Sir Neville cleared his throat and blinked back tears that were threatening to form. "We have a special present here for her today, and with thanks to Molly Sykes for bringing her to the Hog and Frog especially for this moment, would you both please come forward."

Holding the hand of a young blonde girl dressed in a floral dress and jandals, Molly navigated her way from the back, past the chairs to the front where they stood facing Santa on the far side of the group around the wheelchair.

"Are you really Santa?' asked the girl. There was a ripple of laughter from the audience.

"Well, that depends," said Sir Neville, the child's eyes grew wide and her mouth formed an O. "Do you believe I can give you a Christmas miracle?" he asked. The child hesitated and then nodded.

"What do you want more than anything?" asked Sir Neville.

"For my Mum to be better and to go home with her," she answered. Her small face determined.

"Well, I think we can do that. Nurse Kipps, would you like to show Nicki who you have with you today?" The wheelchair was turned to face Molly and Nicki.

It took less than a second for Nicki to recognise her mother and let out a squeal of delight and ran to her, falling into her arms, and for the first time they saw Nicki sobbing.

"For those who don't know, Nicki has been staying with Molly Sykes while her mother was in a coma after a tragic accident. A few days ago she woke up and has been working hard to get her strength back so she was able to see Nicki again. This is the first time since the accident that Nicki has seen her mother out of a coma. We want her to know what a delight Nicki has been in the town and three people she has touched want to tell you. Mrs West, would you like to go first?"

She told the stories of keeping young Hemi and the young foster boy Ford, in line and teaching them both the joy of reading and that family does matter no matter what that family is, by blood or by circumstance. Molly added to that and soon there were a few sobs coming from the audience.

Next was Ms. Hill, local teacher who had Nicki in her class, then it was Bob's turn. He cleared his throat.

"Nicki is my Christmas miracle," he started. "I've had my ups and downs lately. The broken leg knocked me more than I realised and now my family, my 'minders' are no longer here," there were a few chuckles from those who knew Bob.

"I found I would be on my own for Christmas. I was a bit down, and at my low point Nicki entered. Together we put together this year's Christmas Garden, and you're all invited to view the wonderful display." Bob seemed a stand a little taller, shoulders back with a look of joy talking about the garden.

"I have to acknowledge Lou as well, her sense of colour is much better than mine, so it's the best display ever. Just don't expect as good next year if I don't get help from those two again. A ripple of laughter went around the room.

"By doing this with Nicki, my spirits picked up. I started to think of her as a granddaughter and I want to thank her mother for raising such a wonderful child."

Applause erupted from everyone gathered, and calls of 'well done' and 'good job'.

Sir Neville pulled a handkerchief from his pocket and wiped away tears. This sort of thing always got to him.

"Nicki's mum, Pamela Poppy Beattie, Pam, we have great pleasure in providing you with a small rental property here in Thornbury and my trust will help pay for all your ongoing medical and legal costs." A sob came from Pam's lips causing Nicki to become concerned. Calming her daughter she turned to Sir Neville, with a crocked smile.

"How can I ever repay you?" asked Pam in a slurred rasping voice.

"Just get better, and with Nicki's attitude, she'll be helping you get there quicker than you think."

The room erupted with chatter and laughter, Sarah went over to Sir Neville and stood next to him.

"That was a lovely thing to do," she said, "you have such a good heart." Sir Neville smiled. The time was right.

"Ladies and Gentlemen, I have one more announcement." His voice boomed out over the gathering and everyone became quiet.

"I am not getting any younger," there was some laughter, "and my doctor is concerned with my health." There were oohs from the room.

Sarah turned and looked at Sir Neville, her brows knitted and she was about to say something but he stopped her by taking her hand.

"This is something I've been planning for some time and today is the day. Today I want to formally acknowledge that I am Sarah's biological father," there was a gasp from the room and Sarah almost fell over, it was only because Sir Neville was holding onto her that she didn't. Julie rushed to Sarah's side to hold her other hand.

"I expect many of you older residents suspected it for years," he smiled. "I now have an heir, and in this envelope are the documents for Sarah to take over my business, assuming she wants it of course. But I cannot think of safer hands for it to go to. Sarah has been part of my life since she was born and my wonderful personal assistant since, oh, I can't remember, a long time." Another ripple of laughter.

"All I ask of her is that the Children's Christmas party and this Christmas Day lunch continue. As Sarah does most of the work organising it, I doubt she'd find it difficult." He gave her a cheeky grin and she shook her head, even though she was smiling. "I also ask that I get to be Santa, while I'm able."

"Of course," said Sarah, recovering from the initial shock, "who else would we get?"

She would have given him a hug, but for now he was still her employer, and even though she knew there was some family relationship between them, she never imagined he was her father. But it all made sense in an odd way.

She hoped they'd spend some time over the next few days to talk this over. Taking on the Emerson Corporation and Foundations was a monumental responsibility. She had to make sure she was ready for it.

He felt lighter, as if a great weight was lifted. Today was a happy day and he'd talk to Sarah and Julie about his MS diagnosis later, when they were alone. For today was Christmas day and the promise of good things to come.

After the Party

At the back of the room, on her own, Mags Wild sat alone at a table, a glass of bubbles in front of her. She gulped it down and took the glass to the bar.

"Any more?" asked Mags, as Ross came over to her.

"Sure, Ms. Wild," said Ross and he came back with an open bottle that was just under half full. "Want to take the bottle? You look like you've had a bit of a shock." He handed over the bottle. Mags took it with a quick smile and thanks, then went back to her seat.

The room was thinning out as people headed home or out for a walk now that the afternoon had turned out fine and bright. Mags wanted a friend, but Bob was busy talking with Sir Neville and Mark, Nettie was with her friend Beth and there wasn't anyone else she wanted to talk to.

She poured herself another glass and gulped it down, then emptied the rest of the bottle into the glass. She sat looking at it wondering what to do next. She didn't feel like going home right now, the day had been … well … unsettling.

Then she remembered her present sat unopened in her bag and while she decided now was as good a time as any to open it.

She picked up her bag and was about to rummage though it when she noticed the envelope from Aunt Barbara sitting at the top. She placed it on the table and bit her top lip while deciding what she should do about it.

She looked around the room, there were only a few people now. Both Nettie and Bob had gone, she felt a little let down. With a little wave, Molly walked past her table with Nicki, Mags waved back. Looking down at the envelope, if all of this were true, and there was no reason to think it wasn't, then she was a biological grandmother. It was hard to digest, she shook her head.

"Hello" said a husky voice next to her. Mags looked up and saw Pam in front of her.

"Oh, hello," replied Mags, thinking this could be awkward.

"May I sit?" asked the Nurse and Mags nodded.

"I saw you go up, for your present," said Pam, she spoke slowly trying not to slur her words. "I think … I was told …" She hesitated, took a deep breath and continued "You might be my mother."

There it was, Mags took a sudden intake of breath, she wasn't expecting someone to come out with it just like that. Then she nodded, "I was told you are my daughter, but I only found out this week."

Pam gave a crooked smile, "I only found out this week too." She took a paper out of her pocket that was a photocopy of the birth certificate Mags had in the envelope.

"You kept the name Poppy?" said Mags, she'd heard Sir Neville use her full name and a spark of joy was kindled.

Pam nodded, "When I found out that was my birth name, it seemed just right. I was born on ANZAC day."

"I know" smiled Mags, "I was there," she added.

"Oh," said Pam until it dawned on her what that meant and she let out a laugh.

"Nicki is lovely," said Mags, wondering what to say next. "Bob is really taken with her. I hope I can get to know her." Mags stopped. Where did that come from? She still didn't know if she wanted them to be in her life, she was still coming to terms with it after all these years of suppressing the memory.

"We'd love to have you in our lives," said Pam, "I think it will help me get better, knowing I have a family and a future now."

That was an odd statement Mags thought, she wondered what it meant. She knew nothing of this woman, of her child or their circumstances. Where was her husband, or at least Nicki's father? But it didn't feel right to ask right now.

"How did you find out?" asked Mags.

Pam cocked her head on one side and just for a moment, Mags could see a likeness to her brother.

"When Mrs Sykes came to see me, and tell me Nicki was reluctant to visit, I felt my world had truly shattered. It was the only thing that was keeping me going. Waiting to see Nicki. I burst into tears and told her I had nowhere to go when I was well enough to leave the hospital. It was worrying me." Pam wiped her eyes.

Mags looked at the young woman in front of her, she could see parts of her brother, her mother and … him. She wondered what had become of him for a brief second then shook her head. Not now!

"I had nowhere for us to stay," continued Pam, "and I asked if she could keep looking after Nicki until I found somewhere to live. She came back the next day with Sir Neville. We talked about what had happened, I signed a paper for him and said he'd see what he could do. He came back a couple of days later with a woman named Barbara." Mags gasped.

"Aunt Barbara? But why?"

"She is the owner of the small rental property," replied Pam. Mags was surprised, she didn't know Aunt Barbara owned property in the town.

"We were talking and then she started asking me about my parents." Pam stopped and seemed to struggle to breath. The nurse gave her a bottle of water and a small white pill which she took with the water. They waited for a minute or so until Pam was ready to speak again.

"Anyway, we were talking and I told her my parents had kicked me out when I went off with Nicki's father, that it didn't matter because I was adopted. Then she asked if I wanted to know about my birth mother." She took a few deep breaths, as if struggling to get air in her lungs, then took another gulp of water.

"I said yes, she gave me that paper. Then she left. I had a name and that was all. I didn't know you were here." Pam's breathing became laboured and the nurse stood up.

"I think we'd better get you back to the hospital, too much fun is starting your asthma up."

"I'd like to get to know you," said Pam as the nurse started wheeling her away from the table. "Would you come and visit me?"

"Yes," said Mags smiling but also feeling apprehensive, "I'd like that." She watched as the nurse wheeled her daughter away. She tried to work out what she felt, but at the moment it was nothing. Maybe in a few hours it would make sense, but right now she was on her own, going home to her house, where she'd be alone.

A small niggling feeling started at her, and she knew she needed to talk, there was too much information to take in and she really wanted to talk it through. There were only a few people she felt like talking to right now, Aunt Barbara and Bob, and maybe Nettie but she had a visitor staying, so talking with her would have to wait.

Walking home, she felt the world starting to spin out of control; this was unlike her, normally she met any challenge head on. But this was different, very different. What would she do?

Letting herself into her house, the quiet emptiness got to her. She sat at the kitchen table with tears streaming down her face. She looked in her bag for the cellphone number her aunt had given her and called it. Aunt Barbara answered it immediately. A sense of calm or it could have been relief, washed over Mags. Everything would be ok now. She'd talk to Aunt Barbara, and then she'd have to tell Bob. But that would be another day. For now, she had to come to terms with the enormity of the day.

As Aunt Barbara said, she had to take it one step at a time.

*"Sometimes good things fall apart so better things
can fall together."*

- Marilyn Monroe

Christmas Recipes

I love the smell of Christmas trees, singing Christmas carols, baking my family's favourite cookies, wrapping presents, and decorating my house!

- Debbie Trafton O'Neal

Bob's Christmas Sweet Treats

Aunt Helen's Chocolate Truffles

White Christmas

Coffee and Walnut Fudge

Marzipan Treats

Christmas Tree decoration

Aunt Barbara's Star Biscuits

Aunt Helen's Chocolate Truffles

375 g dark chocolate

200 g butter

½ packet pitted prunes (orange flavoured for something different)

¼ cup port

3 cups icing sugar

2 extra blocks of chocolate for dipping

Method

1. Melt the chocolate and butter over a pan of hot water.

2. Cut the prunes up with kitchen scissors and put in the microwave with the port on high for 2 - 3 minutes.

3. Mix all the above with the icing sugar.

4. Put the mix in the fridge to chill until firm but not solid.

5. Remove from the fridge and roll into small balls. Put them on foil lined trays and freeze.

6. Melt the blocks of chocolate for dipping over hot water.

7. Dip the balls in the melted chocolate and allow to set.

Once covered, store in air-tight container. Do not store in the fridge or freezer.

White Christmas

2 ½ cups rice bubbles

1 cup desiccated coconut

1 cup mixed dried fruit

¼ cup each of green and red glace cherries

1 cup icing sugar

½ cup powdered milk

250 g vegetable shortening

80 g dark chocolate

Method

1. Place rice bubbles, coconut, fruit and cherries in a bowl. Chop white chocolate roughly and add to the bowl, then add the icing sugar and milk powder.

2. Melt the vegetable shortening and pour into the rice bubble mixture. Mix well to combine.

3. Press mixture into a baking paper lined 20 cm by 30 cm sponge roll tin. Set in the refrigerator until solid.

4. Melt dark chocolate and drizzle the top. Leave to set. Cut into cubes.

Coffee and Walnut Fudge

75 g butter

1 Tbsp instant coffee, dissolved in 1 Tbsp boiling water

1 Tbsp coffee liqueur

500 g icing sugar

1 Tbsp cream

½ cup coarsely chopped walnuts, lightly toasted

Method

1. Place the butter, coffee dissolved in boiling water and liqueur in a deep microwave proof bowl. Heat for 1 – 2 minutes until the butter is melted. Stir well/

2. Sift the icing sugar in and mix well. Stir in the cream and walnuts.

3. Pour into a tray lined with waxed paper. Refrigerate to set. Cut into squares.

Marzipan Treats

200 g marzipan

1 cup mixed dried fruit

¼ tsp almond essence

1 tsp mixed spice

Icing sugar for sprinkling

Cinnamon for sprinkling

Chocolate for melting

Method

1. Soften marzipan and mix dried fruit, almond essence and spice into the marzipan.

2. Shape into 30cm x 4 cm wide log shape. Cut into slices.

3. Dip part or all of the slice into melted chocolate. Sprinkle for effect depending on taste with icing sugar and/or cinnamon.

"Christmas now surrounds us, Happiness is everywhere. Our hands are busy with many tasks as carols fill the air."

- Shirley Sallay

Aunt Barbara's Star Biscuits

125 g butter

¾ cup caster sugar

1 egg

1 tsp vanilla essence

2 cups flour, sifted

Icing:

1 cup icing sugar

2 tsp butter

2 drops vanilla essence

Silver balls

Fine ribbon to attach biscuits

Method

1. Pre-heat oven to 180 deg. C and prepare two baking trays.

2. Beat butter and sugar until light and creamy. Add egg and beat well. Add vanilla.

3. Add flour and mix to a soft dough. Shape dough into a ball. Cover and refrigerate for 30 minutes.

4. Roll mixture out to a thickness of 5 mm. Using a star shaped biscuit cutter, stamp shapes from the dough. Place on baking trays. With a skewer, make a small hole in one point of each biscuit. Bake for 10 minutes until golden. Transfer biscuits to a wire rack to cool.

5. To make the icing – place the icing sugar, butter and vanilla in a small bowl. Add sufficient water to mix to a thick smooth consistency.

6. Decorate biscuits with icing and silver balls. Allow the icing to dry before threading ribbon through the hole in each biscuit. To keep the biscuits fresh, cover with cellophane before hanging them from the Christmas tree.

*Christmas is a special time of year when
family and tradition blend together into
magical holiday grandeur.*

Connect with me:

 In the *Netties Knit Shop Series*:

Secrets of the Wool

A Tisket A Tasket

Died with Flowers

Lost Angels – A short story – kindle only

Christmas at the Hog and Frog

Anthologies Love Wounds – stories from 'A Writers Plot'

Visit – **https://www.cblandyauthor.com/**

Sign up to my newsletter for up-to-date information on releases,

Bob's recipes and other fun stuff -

https://www.cblandyauthor.com/contact.html

Follow on Facebook - https://www.facebook.com/CBLandyauthor/

About the author:

Supported by two black and white cats, the bees on B deck, and a wonderful husband; CB Landy has been attending writing groups over the last ten years and working with wonderful people to develop her voice as an author.

As a writer, CB Landy's motto is - Life is too short to read and write about the woes of the world, we have the world news for that.

Avid reader, passionate about great stories and storytelling, a perfect day would be sitting in the sun reading the latest purchase, usually a cozy mystery, historical mystery or paranormal hi-jinx.

Her stories are light, fun and reflect small town New Zealand and the wonderful people you meet there.